GETTING AIR

Also by DAN GUTMAN

The Homework Machine
Race for the Sky
Back in Time with Benjamin Franklin
Back in Time with Thomas Edison

GETTING AIR
Dan Gutman

Simon & Schuster Books for Young Readers
New York London Toronto Sydney

SIMON & SCHUSTER BOOKS FOR YOUNG READERS
An imprint of Simon & Schuster Children's Publishing Division
1230 Avenue of the Americas, New York, New York 10020
This book is a work of fiction. Any references to historical events, real people, or real locales are used fictitiously. Other names, characters, places, and incidents are products of the author's imagination, and any resemblance to actual events or locales or persons, living or dead, is entirely coincidental.
Copyright © 2007 by Dan Gutman
All rights reserved, including the right of reproduction in whole or in part in any form.
SIMON & SCHUSTER BOOKS FOR YOUNG READERS is a trademark of Simon & Schuster, Inc.
Book design by Daniel Roode
The text for this book is set in Horley Old Style MT.
Manufactured in the United States of America
2 4 6 8 10 9 7 5 3 1
Library of Congress Cataloging-in-Publication Data
Gutman, Dan.
Getting air / Dan Gutman.—1st ed.
p. cm.
Summary: After foiling a terrorist hijacking aboard their plane, fourteen-year-old Jimmy, his younger sister, and two skateboarding friends crash-land the plane and try to survive in a forest wilderness until help arrives.
ISBN-13: 978-0-689-87680-6
ISBN-10: 0-689-87680-7
[1. Wilderness survival—Fiction. 2. Survival—Fiction.] I. Title.
PZ7.G9846Gh 2007
[Fic]—dc22
2006032690

FIRST
EDITION

To my son, Sam, who inspired my whole career.
Thanks to Bill Freeman and Dick Barton, and to
Gary Paulsen for writing *Hatchet*.

I never wanted to be a hero. All I ever wanted to be was a Woodpusher.

                              -Jimmy Zimmerman

CHAPTER 1:
The First 1080

This is my ultimate fantasy . . .

I hear the crowd starting to buzz and clap and stamp their feet as I climb the inside steps to the fourteen-foot halfpipe. It's a long way up. I give my helmet and elbow pads one last tug, mostly for good luck.

It's the X Games and the whole world is watching. Or the whole skateboarding world, anyway. Dozens of other kids have had their turn and I go last. Because I'm the best, right? I'm the one they all came to see. Finally I reach the top of the halfpipe just as the announcer yells . . .

". . . and last but not least, from Livingston,

New Jersey, the thirteen-year-old phenom who has taken the extreme sports world by storm, Jimmy . . . Zimmerman!"

The crowd goes wild, of course. My sister, Julia, and my lifelong friends, Henry and David, are there, shouting encouragement and telling me how awesome I am.

I look around Madison Square Garden and wave. A thousand flashes blind me momentarily. But I know why I'm there. I know what I have to do to win this thing. I have to land the first 1080.

Nobody ever did three complete revolutions in the air before and came down with both feet on their board. *Ever*. Some big shot scientists claimed it wasn't possible. Even I, the incredible Jimmy Zimmerman, never landed a 1080. Not even in practice. But I was going to go for it here. Because that's the kind of skater I am. Go for broke. Risk it all. Second place isn't good enough.

The crowd quiets to a hush as I hang most of my board off the edge of the coping. I put one foot on the tail to steady the board.

"I love you, Jimmy!" shouts a voice in the crowd.

I look around until I spot her, supermodel Victoria Ashley, my girlfriend and quite possibly the most gorgeous girl in the world. I flip her a wink and throw a thumbs up. Like it's no sweat.

I take a peek down. It looks like forever. There are about three feet of straight vert before the halfpipe begins curving out. It's even scarier when you're standing at the edge. You feel like you're about to jump off the ledge of a building. But I've dropped into hundreds of halfpipes. This is a piece of cake to me.

I take a few deep breaths, put my other foot on the front of the board and lean forward. Just about anybody who's crazy enough can drop into a fourteen-foot halfpipe. It's what you do once you're in there that matters.

I slide down smoothly and bend my knees to roll up the opposite wall almost to the top. Then I turn and do it again, pumping my legs to get air on the other side. As I pop over the coping, I spin one revolution, just to tease the crowd.

"Three-sixty!" they scream.

I come down fakie and shoot up the other side, spinning two revolutions in the air. I can fly.

"Seven-twenty!" they scream.

That was easy. I slide down again and now I'm a few feet over the top. There's time for two-and-a-half revolutions, and then I roll down.

"Nine hundred!" they scream.

But the nine hundred has been done before. I know everyone is moving to the edge of their seat now. They want to watch history being made. They want to be able to tell their children and their grandchildren they were there when Jimmy Zimmerman landed the first 1080. Or when I busted my head trying.

I'm focused. I'm in the zone. It feels like I'm moving in slow motion. I do a couple more back and forths to work up my air and work up my courage. I throw in a kickflip-indy and a tail-grab to build a little tension with the crowd. To show 'em what else I've got.

In order to complete three revolutions, I'm going to need to spin early, fast, and tight. As I roll up the wall, I launch myself, holding one arm against my body and holding my board below me with the other hand.

One . . .

Two . . .

Two and a half . . .

Three!

And I stick it, both feet on the board. I steady myself, then throw my arms in the air and the crowd is nuts. Camera flashes light up the Garden like lightning.

"He did it!" the announcer booms. "For the first time in history, a human being has spun three complete revolutions in the air and landed on a skateboard! Let's hear it for Jimmy Zimmerman!"

When I come out of the halfpipe, kids are swarming all over me for autographs. I take off one sneaker, throw it into the crowd, and a bunch of fans climb all over each other to get it. I step up on the podium with the two guys who came in second and third. Somebody gives me my first-place trophy and a big check. I'm surrounded by reporters and guys in suits who were sent by skateboard companies to sign me to multimillion-dollar sponsorship deals.

But there will be plenty of time for that later. Right now, Victoria is coming over to give me a kiss.

Here she is. I open my arms.

And then, my ultimate fantasy comes to an end when my brand-new titanium skateboard falls on my head.

CHAPTER 2:
Boarding

"Oh my gosh! Are you okay? Your skateboard doesn't seem to fit in the overhead bin. If it doesn't fit under the seat in front of you, I guess you'll have to hold it on your lap. Do you need some ice for your head?"

I looked up at the flight attendant. It was like I was in a different fantasy. She was tall, with wavy blond hair and green eyes. She spoke with a gentle Southern accent. At first I thought she was part of a video game. Nobody in the real world could look that beautiful. The little pin on her uniform said ARCADIA. There was another flight attendant on the other side of the plane, but she was closer to my mom's age. Me and the guys lucked out. I memorized the pretty flight attendant's name. *Arcadia Maisonette.*

"I'm okay," I replied, rubbing my head.

"Skateboarding really *is* dangerous!" Arcadia said before walking past me to the back of the plane. I wasn't sure if she was joking or not.

"I think I'm in love," I whispered to my little sister Julia, who was sitting next to me, her head stuck in a book, like always. She's eleven. I gave Julia the window seat so I wouldn't have to look out of it. But I claimed the middle armrest, because I'm older. She didn't fight me for it, because she knows I can take her, easy.

"The minimum age to be a flight attendant is eighteen," Julia said, without taking her eyes off the page. "That would make her at least five years older than you."

"I don't care," I insisted. "When we're sitting

on the porch in our retirement community fifty years from now, it won't matter. What difference does age make when you're in love?"

Julia rolled her eyes and returned to her book. It was called *Hatchet*. I read that book a few years ago in school. It's about some kid who's in a plane crash. Good airplane reading.

I looked out the window. We were in one of those small jets with an engine mounted on either side in the back by the tail, not on the wing. I never trusted those planes with the engines hanging off the wings. What if the engines fall off?

"Hey, Zimmerman, you should ask that stewardess out on a date," whispered my friend Henry, who was sitting in the seat behind me. "She's hot!"

"Are you crazy?" I replied. "She's probably five years older than me."

Henry and David were in 17A and B, right

near that place where they keep the drinks and snacks. What's it called? The galley? I don't like sitting in the back row, because you can't lean your seat back.

I turned around to check on Henry. He had never even been away from home before and I was afraid he might freak out on the plane or something. He seemed to be doing fine. Sitting by the window and next to Henry, David was chewing gum. He was wearing one of those funny-looking eye masks. How can anyone sleep on an airplane? There's so much to worry about.

Arcadia and the other flight attendant had moved to the front, and they were pointing out the location of the emergency exits. I wondered if you have a better chance of surviving a crash in the back of the plane or the front? I mean, if the plane hits something, the people in the front are sure to get crushed right away. But the people in the back will probably be burned alive or die from smoke inhalation.

This is the kind of stuff that goes through my head when I'm flying. Why couldn't they have put us on one of those jumbo jets? This thing couldn't hold more than sixty or seventy passengers. I wondered if the jumbos were safer than these little jets.

"I wish we were driving," I said to nobody in particular, knowing full well that none of us was old enough to get a license. It would take weeks to drive cross-country anyway.

"Do you know how many Americans die every year in car accidents?" Julia asked me.

"How many?"

"Forty thousand, on average," she said. "And do you how many die in plane crashes?"

"I give up."

"Two hundred," she said.

How does she know stuff like that? My kid sister has probably read the whole library. She needs to get a life. Julia is the queen of useless information. At her school, kids call her TP, for "Trivial Pursuit."

Those statistics can't be right. Nobody can tell me that being in a car on the ground is more dangerous than being 30,000 feet up in the air in a giant aluminum tube weighing hundreds of thousands of pounds that's moving 500 miles an hour. I'll never figure out how they get the thing off the ground. It's like magic.

At least I have a seat belt. I chuckled to myself. Yeah, like a seat belt is gonna do any good if we go down.

We would be making a connection in Chicago, and then out to California for two weeks. Julia and I have cousins who live in Newport Beach. They promised to take us to the X Games, which are in Los Angeles this year. Henry and David talked their folks into letting them come with us.

The three of us started a skateboard club back in third grade. Most of the kids in our class were into the traditional team sports, but after watching the X Games on TV one day, we were hooked. We went out and bought skateboards right away, those cheap ones they sell at Toys "R" Us. We practiced constantly, and as we got better we got better equipment. We got to be pretty good.

New Jersey is not exactly what you'd call a hotbed of skateboarding. We discovered right away that the in-line skaters and BMX bikers didn't like us, for no particular reason. It was like they were prejudiced because we rode skateboards. Henry started making fun of them by calling them "fruit booters" and "seat humpers." We were equally hated by the football players ("brain bashers"), the baseball players ("bat whackers"), and the hockey players ("puck junkies").

They had a name to make fun of us too. *Woodpushers*. At first we were insulted. It was sort of like a racial slur. But after a while the name sort of grew on us. Woodpushers. We started liking it. So when we decided to form the club, there was only one name we considered— the Woodpushers.

Our plan was to try and get sponsored while we were in L.A. Every skateboard company would be at the X Games, and they're always looking for fresh talent, new faces. It was a long shot, of course. We all knew that. There are a million skateboarders out there who were just as good as us. Probably better. But you know what they say—you gotta be in it to win it. Me and Henry and David are the All-American boys. We're not punks. We're not into piercing and death metal and all that. Skateboard companies should love us. If nothing else, maybe they'd give us some free T-shirts and decks and stuff. We'll take anything.

It's hard to get sponsored when you live in New Jersey and all the action is on the West Coast. Last year we borrowed a video camera from David's dad and made a cool skate video *(Woodpushers Gone Wild)* but it didn't get us anywhere. And we sent that DVD to *ten* skateboard companies. Nobody was interested in the Woodpushers. They probably get DVDs and tapes in the mail every day. I'll bet they never even look at them. You've got to be either really good or really lucky to get sponsored.

My head was still throbbing from the skateboard hitting me. It was brand new. I built the thing myself. Well, my dad actually did most of the work. He used to work for a company that makes lawn furniture. Before they laid him off, Dad brought home an extra piece of titanium alloy to fool around with. We cut it into the shape of a skateboard deck, then we welded trucks on and attached wheels and bearings. With grip tape glued to the top and some stickers on the bottom, it looked just like any ordinary wooden skateboard. Until it slams you on the head, of course.

I hadn't even tried out the new board yet. But it should be awesome because it's just as flexible as wood, but much stronger and lighter. So you should be able to do more tricks with it and beat it up without worrying about it breaking. The thing is virtually indestructible. I told my dad that if he licensed it to one of the big skateboard companies, they'd probably pay him a million dollars. But he said that's crazy talk and he needed to focus on getting a new job. The guys even talked about kicking me out of the Woodpushers because I wasn't pushing wood anymore. Nothing ever came of that.

Julia doesn't skateboard. She's more into Girl Scouts and reading. Me and Henry and

David live to skate. We even built a halfpipe in David's backyard. Henry downloaded the plans off the Internet and we all chipped in to buy the wood at Home Depot. It was a small halfpipe, but pretty cool. At least it was until it rained a few times and the wood got warped and ruined. I guess we should have covered it or shellacked it or something. But after we finished building it, all we wanted to do was skate. Anyway, we got a few good months out of the halfpipe before the boards started to pop up and it became unskateable.

The plane wasn't close to being full, but I figured all the passengers were on because that cute flight attendant, Arcadia, was closing the door. Soon we'd be taking off.

"Young man, can you help me for a moment?"

It was a little old lady who was sitting in Row 15 in front of me. She looked like my grandmother and she talked with a British accent.

"Sure."

"I need to put my sweater in the overhead bin but I can't quite reach that high."

As I got up to help the lady, I looked around. There were a few other guys on the plane. But besides them, and me, Julia, Henry, and David, the plane was just about filled with old ladies. I had never seen so much gray hair in one place at one time. A few of them looked like they had *blue* hair. Or maybe it was purple. It was definitely not a color found in nature. Henry calls old ladies "Mildreds" because it seems like all of them are named Mildred.

I helped the lady put her sweater away. The Mildred sitting next to her was knitting. Knitting? I thought that was just something old ladies did in the movies. I didn't think anyone actually did it in real life. I wondered how they got their knitting needles past security. I didn't even bring my nail clipper on board with me because I was afraid it would be confiscated. I guess when you're an old lady, you can get away with more stuff.

"Thank you very much, young man," she said. "What's your name?"

"Jimmy Zimmerman."

"Mildred Herschel," she said, sticking out a bony hand.

Figured. Man, it must have been confusing back when those old ladies were young and all the girls were named Mildred.

I shook Mrs. Herschel's hand. I figured that would be the end of it, but she didn't let go of my hand. So I had to say something.

"Do you like to knit?" I asked. What a stupid thing to say. I never know what to say to old ladies.

"Oh, yes!" Mrs. Herschel said. "My group and I are going to a knitting convention in California. We go every year."

They actually have knitting conventions? I
guess old ladies have to do *something* to pass the
time. She *still* wouldn't let go of my hand.

"Me and my friends are skateboarders," I told
her. "We're going to L.A. to get sponsored."

"Sponsored?" Mrs. Herschel asked. "What
does that mean?"

"Well," I told her, "if you're really good, the
skateboard companies give you free stuff and
sometimes even pay you to use their equipment.
I guess they figure kids will see you using the
equipment and they'll buy it hoping it will make
them good."

"I should jolly well think so," Mrs. Herschel
said. "Sometimes the yarn companies give away
samples of their products to the top knitters."

"Maybe you'll get sponsored too," I told her.

"That would be smashing!" she said. "Well,
good luck to you, Jimmy. You seem to be a fine
young man."

"Zimmerman is into *extreme* knitting," Henry piped up from behind me. "A bunch of knitters skydive out of an airplane and they knit a parachute on the way down. They have to work really *fast*."

Henry is such a dork.

Mrs. Herschel laughed and said Henry was cheeky, whatever that means. I sat back down and told Henry what a moron he is.

"Hey, I was trying to do you a favor," Henry whispered. "Maybe *she'll* go out with you. I know how you go for older women."

"Very funny."

Arcadia and the other flight attendant were demonstrating how to buckle the seat belt—as if none of us had ever been in a car before!

"Excuse me," Henry called out. "Can you demonstrate that one more time? My friend Zimmerman here is a little slow. I don't think he quite understands how the locking mechanism works."

I called Henry a dork again. Arcadia smiled in our direction and my heart melted.

"In case of emergency," the other flight attendant announced, "an oxygen mask will drop down over your head. In the unlikely event of a water landing, your seat cushion can be used as a flotation device."

Water landing? We'd be flying over Kansas!

"If this thing lands on anything but a runway, we can kiss our butts good-bye," David said behind me. "Because we'll all be dead."

I searched around in the seat pocket in front of me until I found a set of earphones. Maybe a little music would relax me. I plugged the earphones into the jack on the side of my armrest.

"Cockpit, this is ground crew," a voice said. "Our pre-departure checks are complete. Standing by for pushback clearance."

"Roger, stand by for pushback clearance."

"United 39, you are cleared to position, hold on runway four left."

"United 39, you're cleared for takeoff, runway four left."

Arcadia was coming down the aisle with a tray, passing out little bags of pretzels. I took off the earphones and desperately tried to think of something clever to say to her. She was almost upon me.

"Do you like pretzels?" I asked as she handed me a bag. What an idiot I am.

"Yes, but I like the big soft ones better," she replied, "with mustard on them. That's the way they eat them in Philadelphia."

"Sounds delicious," I agreed, even though the thought of putting mustard on a pretzel made me nauseous.

"Smooth," whispered Henry when Arcadia walked back toward the front. "Now I know why the chicks dig you so much, Zimmerman."

I am so lame. If it was the movies, I would have said something really cool and Arcadia would have fallen in love with me on the spot. Then we'd be at the airport waiting to get on separate planes and she'd run to me because she couldn't bear the thought of living the rest of her life without me.

I started to work on a fantasy in which Arcadia and I were married. She'd give up being a flight attendant so she could travel around the world with me to my skateboarding competitions. Sometimes we'd fly off to tropical islands to pose for swimsuit calendars.

My fantasy was just starting to get interesting when I felt the plane rolling. We had pushed away from the gate. I could see the airport out the window as the pilot steered us onto the runway.

We didn't have to wait long. Soon the plane was building up speed. Everything was shaking, but when the wheels lifted off the ground, it suddenly got smooth and quiet.

I gripped the armrest tightly and closed my eyes. My stomach felt like it was falling away.

"Don't worry," Julia assured me after we were in the air. "Seventy percent of all plane crashes take place on the takeoff or the landing. Takeoff looks fine, so our chances just got a lot better."

"Oh, thanks a lot," I said.

Somebody left a find-a-word puzzle magazine in the seat pocket. I started looking at it, but I didn't have a pencil. I couldn't concentrate anyway. I picked up the card with a cartoon on it that tells you what to do if there's an emergency. It didn't hold my attention. I had a Game Boy, but the pilot said we had to turn off all electronic devices. I wished I could go to sleep and just wake up in California.

"Hey, check it out!" Henry said. He had poked holes in his barf bag and made it into a hand puppet. Henry even drew a little face on it.

"If you feel sick, throw up into me!" he said in a funny voice.

"Most amusing," I told him.

I flipped to a few of the channels on the earphones, but all they played was lame elevator music that old people listened to in the last century. Good music to knit by. I guess that stuff is supposed to be soothing.

The video screens dropped down from the ceiling and the pilot told us he was going to show a movie, some chick flick starring Gwyneth Paltrow. Lucky I had a barf bag in case I caught a glimpse of it.

"Hey, did you ever notice they never have in-flight movies with plane crashes in them?" I announced to nobody in particular.

"Yer a foon, Zimmerman," David said from behind me.

"A foon?" I asked. "What's a foon?"

"A foon is a fool with an *N* in it, you foon," David said.

"Oh, of course. Everybody knows that."

"We're not gonna crash, Zimmerman," David said. "So pipe down or we'll all beat the carp out of you."

"Carp?" I asked. "Don't you mean crap?"

"No, I mean carp," David said. "Reverse the letters."

"I'll beat the carp out of *you*, man," I told David.

"Not in this lifetime, Zimmerman."

At that moment, I heard a scream.

CHAPTER 3:
The Plan

I turned toward the sound of the scream, but I didn't see anything unusual. There was a thud, like the sound of a body hitting the floor. Then more screams. I craned my neck to see what was going on, but I was still belted into my seat. I couldn't see much.

"Somebody probably ralphed their breakfast," David said.

"What the—" Henry said.

"It's the stewardess!" somebody shouted. "We need a doctor!"

All the old ladies were screaming. Suddenly, a guy stood up. He was wearing a mask.

"Don't move!" he shouted.

"Oh my God!" David said. "We're being hijacked!"

My sister grabbed my hand. I grabbed hers. My heart started racing.

Another guy wearing a mask stood up about ten rows in front of us. This guy had something strapped to his waist. A box, it looked like. A bomb? There were at least two hijackers. Maybe more in the first-class section. I couldn't see up there.

"Stabbed!" somebody yelled.

"I think she's dead!" one of the old ladies shouted. "The stewardess is *dead!*"

The first hijacker slapped the lady in the face, then shouted, "Do as we say or you'll be dead too!"

He had an accent. I couldn't place it.

Arcadia, the flight attendant, broke down in tears.

"She's my friend!" she sobbed.

"Sit down and shut up!" the guy with the bomb strapped to his waist ordered. Neither of the hijackers looked much bigger than any of us. They might have been twenty, twenty-five years old.

For a minute, I was just stunned. My heart was thumping and I was sweating all over. This was so far from anything that I ever expected to happen to me. I was paralyzed. I think we all were. At least for a time.

You get on a plane and you expect to fly somewhere. You expect somebody to pick you up at baggage claim and your life continues as it was in some other place. You don't expect some lunatics to take over the plane.

I put my arm around Julia. We don't always get along. But if these guys so much as touched my little sister, I would kill them. I didn't know how, but I would. Julia had already taken my cell phone out of my backpack and was frantically pushing the buttons.

"I can't get a signal!" she said.

"We're gonna die," Henry said behind me. "I'm only thirteen years old and I'm gonna die. I never even got the chance to kiss a girl and I'm gonna die. Nobody ever survives a hijacking."

"That's not true—," Julia said, but she stopped because the plane started to dip and roll. It could have been turbulence, but probably not. My guess was that there was a fight going on in the cockpit. There were probably two other hijackers in first class who somehow got into the cockpit. I looked around. Some of the old ladies were sobbing. Some were praying. Some were just paralyzed with fear. Like us.

"It's all over," Henry said softly, and then he started to cry.

"Screw that," whispered David. "We don't

have time to feel sorry for ourselves. We gotta do something."

David had been pretty quiet up until then. But there was determination in his voice.

"What are we gonna do?" I asked.

"Fight *back*," David said. "How many of them are there?"

"Four, I bet," Julia said. "These two guys guarding us, plus there are probably two in first class who rushed the cockpit."

"And there's four of us, including Squirt," David said, nodding toward my sister. "That's an even fight."

But these guys had weapons, and they had already killed somebody. None of us ever killed anybody. None of us ever even *hurt* anybody.

"Let's get them," said Julia, punching one fist into her open palm.

"Don't even think about it," I told her. "I promised Mom and Dad I would take care—"

Julia wouldn't even let me finish the sentence.

"You guys are going to need all the help you can get."

"How do you think they got in the cockpit?" Henry asked. "I thought those doors were supposed to be locked and secure."

"They're smart," Julia said. "They found a way."

"That guy has a bomb," I said. "If they're going to blow the plane up, there's no point charging them. He'll just set it off early. Maybe we should try to reason with them."

"Are you crazy?" David said. "There's no reasoning with these people! They're suicidal. I bet you a million bucks that bomb is phony. He's just using that to keep us away from him."

"They're going to crash the plane into a building," Julia said. "That's what they did on 9/11. I read all about it. I'll bet they're gonna

hit the White House. That's what they were trying to do with the fourth plane on 9/11. But the
passengers fought back and crashed it into a
field in Pennsylvania."

"I can't believe this is happening to us," said
Henry.

"We gotta do something," said Julia. "And
fast."

The plane made a big bump and all the old
ladies screamed. The two hijackers were watching us carefully. They each had a hand in one
pocket. We had to whisper.

"What weapons do they have?" asked
David.

"The bomb," I said.

"The bomb is fake," David said. "That's for
sure. What *else* do they have?"

"No way they could get a gun or knife past
security," Julia said.

"Then how did he kill the stewardess?"

asked Henry. "He must have used something sharp."

"He could have assembled a knife out of smaller pieces after we left the ground," David said.

"They've each got a hand in a pocket," said Julia.

"It could be a bluff," David said. "They could have nothing."

The old lady in front of me, the *real* Mildred who asked me to put away her sweater, leaned toward me.

"My friend, Adeline, said he jammed a pencil into the stewardess's neck!" she whispered.

"A pencil?" David hissed. "They hijacked the plane with a *pencil*!"

"There are about thirty of us and two of them," Julia calculated.

Yeah, but twenty-six of us were heading for a knitting convention. The hijackers were looking in our direction. I could see their eyes even though they were wearing masks. They knew the old ladies weren't likely to put up much of a fight. We were the ones they had to worry about.

The one who killed the flight attendant looked nervous. But crazy nervous. Like he might go nuts and kill one of us just to set an example and keep the rest of us quiet.

Suddenly, the plane started to bank into a right turn. I don't know a whole lot about geography, but I know there are no turns when you're going from New Jersey to Chicago. It's a straight shot.

"Why are we turning?" I asked.

"We're heading back toward the East Coast," Julia said. "Probably to Washington . . . or New York."

Looking to my right out the window, I could see the ground outside. There was a river.

A voice came over the speakers. It sounded

almost mechanical, like he was reading from a script.

"Ladies and gentlemen, this is the pilot. Everything will be okay. Be calm. We are returning to the airport. Nobody will be hurt."

"That's bull," David said.

Some of the old ladies were praying. Others got their cell phones working or were talking on the phones mounted in the back of the seats. The hijackers weren't doing anything to stop them.

"I love you," I heard them saying into the phones.

"The Lord is my shepherd; I shall not want. He maketh me to lie down in green pastures."

"I need you to be happy for the rest of your life."

"He leadeth me beside the still waters. He restoreth my soul."

"Tell your mommy and daddy I love them."

"He leadeth me in the paths of righteousness for his name's sake."

"I'm sorry we argued . . ."

"Yea, though I walk through the valley of the shadow of death, I will fear no evil; for thou art with me."

"Oh God, please help us. I just want to see your face again."

"Help us, Jesus. I don't want to die!"

"I've got to call Mom and Dad," Julia said, trying to get a signal on my cell phone. "They'll know what to do."

"There's no time for that!" David said forcefully. "We need a plan *now*."

"Please remain sitting," announced the 'pilot.' "We have a bomb aboard. The airlines has our demands. Please remain quiet and nobody will be hurt."

Arcadia was standing in the galley, still sobbing about the other flight attendant.

"We're going down," Henry said. "We're all going to die!"

"All they've got is a pencil!" David said, taking off his seat belt. "If you guys are too wussy, I'll go after them myself."

Before David could get out of his seat, the plane started making erratic movements. Climbing and dropping. Slowing down and speeding up. Shaking. Planes weren't built to fly like that, I knew. One of the overhead bins opened and stuff spilled out into the aisle.

"Oh my God!" somebody screamed.

"Be quiet and you will be okay," said the guy with the bomb. "We are returning to the airport. If you try to make any moves, you will endanger yourself and the aircraft."

"Just stay quiet," said the other one. "Don't try to make any stupid moves. We have a bomb. We have weapons. We will use them if we have to."

"He's bluffing," David said. "If he had

weapons, they wouldn't have killed that lady with a pencil."

"Nobody can help us," whispered Julia. "It's up to us."

"Even if we die," Henry said, "maybe we can do something so fewer people will die on the ground."

They were right. We had to do something, and right away.

"Okay, what's the plan?" I asked.

"We can't all rush the cockpit at once," David whispered. "The aisle is too narrow to get by."

"We gotta get past these two guys first," said Julia.

"I'll go after the guy with the bomb," Henry said. "I took karate."

"You took karate for like three weeks, Henry," I reminded him.

"I learned some stuff," Henry said. "If you press on the carotid artery, it cuts off oxygen flow to the brain. It can kill a man in seconds."

"Oh, and you think he's going to just stand there and let you press his carotid artery?" David said. "He'll jam a pencil in *your* neck. Look, here's the plan. Henry and I gang up on the guy with the bomb. Zimmerman, you and Squirt go after the smaller guy. That's two on one. If we can take these two guys out, then we'll charge the cockpit and get the other guys."

It made sense.

"I want to help too."

It was Arcadia, the flight attendant. She was in the galley next to us, fussing with a coffeepot.

"What are *you* going to do?" asked David.

"I'm boiling water," Arcadia said.

"What, you're making *coffee* for them?" David said.

"The water is to *throw* at them!" she said. "Then we can use the food cart as a battering ram to get into the cockpit."

"That's smart," Henry said.

"Hey you, blondie!"

It was the hijacker, the one who didn't have a bomb. "What are you doing back there? Get over here!"

He was coming toward the back of the plane. I could see the pencil in his hand. Maybe he was going to stab Arcadia, just like he stabbed the other flight attendant. I felt like I had to do something. I didn't know what.

My instincts took over. As he passed my seat, I grabbed my skateboard with both hands and swung it up, back, and as hard as I could. I connected with the back of his head. He fell forward and crumpled to the floor.

"Nice shot, Jimmy!" Julia yelled.

The old ladies started cheering.

"What about the plan?" asked Henry.

"Forget the plan," David said. "Let's get the other guy!"

CHAPTER 4:
Fighting Back

I never hit anybody before in my life. Not even in a schoolyard fight. One time this bully told me to meet him in the playground after school, but the gym teacher found out and stopped it before a punch was thrown.

The hijacker I hit with my skateboard was face down on the floor and he didn't look like he was going to be getting up anytime soon. In a way, I almost felt sorry for him. He was hurt bad. Titanium packs a wallop. I didn't see any blood.

"Quick, hit him again, Zimmerman." David told me, "Just to be on the safe side."

"He's already unconscious," I said.

"Here, let *me* do it," David said, grabbing my board. He swung it over his head and smacked the guy good. He wasn't moving.

Well, that sure improved the odds. Now there was just one hijacker guarding us all in the coach section. There were three of us, my sister, Arcadia, and a bunch of very angry knitters.

The plane took another big bump, and everybody screamed. It occurred to me that the hijacker I hit over the head was lucky, in a way. He wouldn't be awake when we crashed.

"That was a big mistake, little man," said the other hijacker. He was looking straight at me as he stormed down the aisle. Oh no, this was it.

But he didn't get within ten feet of me.

"Get him!" one of the old ladies shouted.

At that, they all jumped out of their seats. Every one of those blue-haired ladies. They went after the guy with knitting needles, canes, umbrellas, and their own fists. Punching, hitting, kicking, pummeling. I had never seen anything like it.

"The time of humiliation is over!" the guy yelled as he struggled to fight the old ladies off. "We will kill you in your own homeland! This is a battle for the sake of God! The ground will shake under your feet! Death to America!"

Arcadia had her coffeepot ready. There was steam coming out of it. She was going to throw the boiling water in the guy's face, but she didn't have to. The old ladies were all over him. We would have piled on to help, but there was no room.

"Kill him!" one of the old ladies shouted.

The guy didn't stand a chance. It was not a pretty sight. He and his pal were both unconscious. The old ladies high-fived each other.

"What do we do now?" I asked. I was gasping for breath. "Maybe we should wait for the other hijackers to come back here and go after them, too."

"They're not gonna come back here," David said. "Not if they know what's good for them. We gotta charge the cockpit. There are probably two of them in there."

"We can't all go in," my sister said.

"I'll go in," one of the old ladies said, brandishing a knitting needle. "I'll kill them both."

"With all due respect, ma'am, I think we have the best chance," said Henry.

"Then go do it," said my friend Mildred, "and hurry!"

She was right. We didn't know where we were. For all we knew, the plane could have been minutes from Washington or New York.

The old ladies went back to their seats, assigning a few of them to watch over the downed hijackers and hit them if they tried to get up. The four of us grabbed canes, needles, anything we could use as a weapon. Henry took a can of soda from the galley so he could punch somebody with it. I got my skateboard. Arcadia put the pot of boiling water on the food cart and we pushed it up the aisle and through the curtain into first class. There was nobody there. The cockpit door was closed.

"You guys will be heroes," Arcadia told us.

"Dead heroes, most likely," mumbled David.

Henry put his arms around me and David. I pulled Julia into the huddle.

"We've been friends since first grade," Henry said quietly. "We'll be Woodpushers forever, no matter what happens."

"Look, forget the touchy-feely carp," David said. "We're probably gonna die. Let's make it so nobody on the ground does."

"We've only got one thing going for us," I said.

"What's that?" Julia asked.

"We don't want to die, and they do."

"Go get 'em, kids!" yelled one of the old ladies.

CHAPTER 5:
Out of Our Minds

The cockpit door was locked, of course. Even if it wasn't, we didn't want to just walk in there. We needed the element of surprise. Our plan was to take the food cart, ram it against the door as hard as we could, and bust it down. Me and David got into position to push, because we were the biggest and strongest.

"Wait a minute!" Arcadia said. "I just remembered. There's a key to the cockpit door! We keep it hidden in the galley in case of emergency!"

"I'd say this qualifies as an emergency," Henry said.

Arcadia rushed back to get the key, stepping over one of the hijackers, who was still out cold. She found it quickly and rushed back.

"Henry, you know a little karate," David said. "You climb in front. Arcadia, you open the lock and then get out of the way so me and Zimmerman can smash the door. As soon as you see one of them, nail him with the water. Right in his face. Then all four of us will go after them. Okay?"

We got into position. I was glad that David was taking charge. Somebody had to. Arcadia slipped the key in the lock and turned it slowly, like she didn't want the hijackers to know we were opening it.

"Okay, on three," David said. "One . . . two . . . three!"

David and I pushed the cart as hard as we could, slamming it against the door full force. It made a big crashing sound, but the door didn't budge.

"Again!" David shouted. "Harder."

But as we pulled the cart back to take another shot, the cockpit door opened. A guy was standing there. He was wearing a mask like the other hijackers and he was holding up an axe. It was one of those emergency axes like the kind firemen use.

"Get out of here!" he yelled. "Return to your seats!"

Like we were really going to do what *he* said! Arcadia chucked the boiling water and nailed him good, right in the kisser. He screamed and dropped the axe while he covered his eyes with his hands.

"Get him!" David shouted.

All four of us charged the guy and beat him with fists, cans, anything we had. He went down fast. His legs were in the cockpit doorway now, so it couldn't have been closed no matter what. We should have grabbed the axe off the floor before we hit him, because the other hijacker who was inside the cockpit picked it up and held it up menacingly.

Behind that guy, I could see that the pilot and copilot were both slumped over at the controls. I couldn't tell if they were alive or not.

"Sit down," the guy ordered us. "Now!"

"I don't *think* so," David said. He grabbed my skateboard out of my hands and swung it at the guy. The guy blocked it with the axe handle. But that gave us an opening. Me and Henry and Julia went after him with everything we had. It was a blur. Confusion. Arms and legs flying. Screaming. Somebody was cut. I saw blood, but I didn't know who it belonged to. I was out of my mind. We all were. We were fighting for our lives.

"The gardens of paradise await!" the guy was screaming as he fought. "The hour of reality approaches! We welcome death and we will all meet in heaven! Eternal bliss will be ours!"

He was nuts. I think it was Henry who hit him with a fire extinguisher, which had been attached to the cockpit wall. He dropped the axe. Then we grabbed him and slammed his head against the wall. He went down, just like his friends.

I was crazy with rage. I couldn't believe what we had done. It was like professional wrestling, but for real. Something instinctive had taken over our minds and compelled us to go crazy for our own survival. I wanted to hit somebody else, but there was nobody else left to hit. We had beaten all four of them.

"Get them out of here!" David yelled. Julia and I dragged the two hijackers out of the cockpit area and onto the floor in first class. The old ladies saw what was going on, and they were cheering.

Were they dead? I wasn't sure. Ordinarily, I would be creeped out touching a dead person. But under the circumstances, I just did what needed to be done and didn't think about it. They were limp and heavy. I had never even *seen* a dead body before. I guess I was experiencing a lot of firsts on this flight. I didn't look at their faces as we dragged them out of the cockpit.

Arcadia said she'd keep an eye on the hijackers and slam them over the head with the coffeepot if any of them woke up. Julia and I rushed back to the cockpit, where Henry and David were.

"He's dead," Henry said, his finger touching the neck of one of the pilots. "No pulse."

Alarms were beeping and nobody was working the controls, but the plane was still flying level. It must have been on autopilot, I guessed. On the floor of the cockpit I noticed an airplane flight manual and a diagram of the cockpit instruments. I wasn't sure if the pilots kept that in the plane or if the hijackers brought it with them to help them fly it.

"What about the other one?" I asked, unsure of which man was the pilot and which was the copilot.

The one who was still slumped over the controls groaned and moved his head a little to look toward us. He was alive! He would be able to land the plane! We were going to live!

"Any of you fellas . . . know how to fly?" the pilot grunted. He was laboring to speak.

"I took a lesson once," Henry said.

"That's gonna have to do," the pilot said softly.

And then his eyes rolled back. He went limp and fell off the seat.

CHAPTER 6:
Final Approach

For a moment, David, Henry, Julia, and I just looked at each other. The pilot was dead. The copilot was dead. All four hijackers were either dead or close to it, laid out on the floor in the cabin behind us. The only people who knew how to fly an airplane were out of commission.

"Do you know anything about flying?" I asked Arcadia. I figured a flight attendant might have picked up a thing or two in her work.

"No!" she replied. Then she called out to the old ladies, "Does anybody know anything about flying?"

"Goodness, no!" one of them said.

A few of the others started praying again. Nobody jumped up and offered to take the controls.

"We gotta land this thing!" David said. "Henry, sit here! Zimmerman, help me drag these guys outta here."

"B-but I just took one lesson!" Henry protested.

His mother always complains that Henry never sticks with anything. He's one of those kids who takes one lesson of something and drops out. Then he takes a lesson of something else and drops out. The good thing is, Henry knows at least a little bit about everything.

"This is Greek to me!" Henry said, his voice rising in panic. He was just sitting there staring at the controls.

"You must have learned *something*," David begged Henry. "Think!"

"I know there's an electrical system, fuel system, navigational system, communications system, fire-detection system, hydraulic system, cabin-pressurization system. But I don't know how to work them!"

I couldn't blame Henry for freaking out. The dashboard or control panel or whatever it was called had dozens of dials and gauges and switches all over it. How could *anyone* know what they all did? Some of the glass covering the dials and gauges had been broken in the fight. Some had blood on them. You couldn't even see through them.

"Okay, calm down, Henry," David said. "Do you remember any of the basics, like how to make the plane go up and down, left and right?"

"Yeah," Henry said, taking a deep breath. "The plane flies straight and level if you don't do anything. You pull on the yoke to go up, and you push it forward to go down. Same with left and right."

I didn't even know what a yoke was, but Henry pulled on some doohickey in front of him that looked like a video game joystick and I could feel the plane tilt up a little.

"That's good, Henry," David said, putting a hand on his shoulder. I knew he was trying to be positive and comforting. Henry was going to need our support.

"It's not like the Cessna I took my lesson in," Henry said. "It's bigger. Heavy. Slow."

"Can you land it?" David asked.

"How should I know?" Henry said, his voice rising again.

"Okay, calm down," David said.

"Where would I land it, anyway?" Henry asked.

It was a good question. We all looked out the window. The plane was pretty low. There was nothing but trees and lakes down there. If there was a highway, maybe we could land on it. But there wasn't. Maybe we were wrong when we thought we had turned back toward the East Coast. Maybe we were flying over Canada.

"The sun is to the right of us," Julia said. "That means we're heading north, toward Canada."

"How do you know?" asked David.

"Girl Scouts," she replied. "The sun rises in the east and sets in the west." Julia has been a scout since she was five. I dropped out of Boy Scouts as soon as I took up skateboarding.

Arcadia came back into the cockpit to check up on us.

"Did you figure out how to make the radio work?" she asked.

The radio! Of course! We could radio somebody and they could "talk us down." I saw somebody do that in a movie once. It hadn't even occurred to me. Henry picked up a headset. He fiddled with it and yelled "Mayday! Mayday!"

"It's busted," he said, "and I think they disabled the transponder."

"The trans*what?*" I asked.

"It's like a receiver that tells the air traffic controllers where we are," Arcadia told me.

"So we're not a blip on some air traffic controller's radar screen?" David asked.

"Possibly not," Arcadia said. "What about fuel? Maybe we can keep flying until we find a better place to land."

We hunted all over for a fuel gauge. There were a few of them on the lower part of the instrument panel. I guess they have more than one fuel tank. The needles were close to empty.

"Oh, great!" David moaned.

That didn't make sense. The plane was heading for Chicago. How could it be low on fuel?

"Maybe the hijackers dumped the fuel," Arcadia said. "You can do that in case you need to get the weight down in an emergency."

"It doesn't make sense," I said. "Why would *they* want to dump fuel?"

"Maybe the *pilot* dumped the fuel as soon as the plane was hijacked," Henry suggested. "That way, the hijackers wouldn't be able to reach their target."

"It doesn't matter who dumped the fuel," David said urgently. "We gotta land this thing soon or we're just gonna run out of gas and go down wherever we are."

He was right. And right after he said that, it suddenly got quieter in the cockpit and the nose started to dip even though Henry hadn't pushed on the yoke.

"What's happened?" I asked.

Henry looked out the left side.

"One of the engines is out!" he shouted.

David cursed.

"Maybe the trees will cushion our fall," Julia said. "Like shock absorbers."

"Yeah, hitting a tree should be real gentle," David said.

"The other engine stopped!" Arcadia shouted, looking out the right side.

We didn't need her to tell us. There was a strange and eerie quiet suddenly. After a while you don't notice the constant hum of an airplane's engine. But when it stops, it's like you're alone in the woods in the middle of the night. It felt like we were moving more slowly.

The nose tilted down a little more. The treetops were suddenly bigger in the window.

"Pull it up, Henry!" David shouted, tapping the fuel gauge with his finger. "We're losing altitude!"

Henry pulled the yoke back and the nose went

up a little, but not all the way to level.

"It won't go any higher!" he yelled. "We're out of fuel. We're gliding!"

"So can you glide it down?" David yelled. "Try to steer it between the trees!"

"It's so heavy!" Henry said, still pulling on the yoke like he was in a tug-of-war.

The trees were getting bigger and bigger, rushing past us. There were trees everywhere. It didn't look like there was any room between them. We had to hit them. We were going awfully fast.

"Hold on!"

"This is it!"

"Brace yourselves against something!" Arcadia yelled.

We probably should have gotten out of the cockpit. We should have run to the back, let the front of the plane hit the trees, and hoped to get out alive after the plane broke apart. That would have been smart. But there was no time. We weren't thinking straight. And we couldn't stop looking at the trees coming at us. It was hypnotizing. We were frozen.

The tops of the trees licked the underside of the plane and there was a scraping noise as they bent against it. Somebody screamed. We were falling into the forest. I saw the nose ram right through the middle of two thick trees. There was a jolt, then a crash. The sound of metal ripping apart. A rush of air. More screams. The smell of something burning. Tree trunks flying past us. Getting knocked off my feet. My head hitting something.

And that was the last thing I remembered.

CHAPTER 7:
Better than the Alternative

I didn't die. I *thought* I had died. How could I have survived? I thought that maybe I was in heaven. That would have been nice, a pleasant way to die. But then I opened my eyes. Heaven probably didn't have the smell of burning rubber. Heaven probably didn't have the wreckage of a small jet plane. That's what I was looking at.

My skateboard was clutched to my chest. Where did that come from? I didn't remember picking it up. But I must have. It was like I was holding on to it for dear life. Maybe it had saved my life. Maybe, like a bulletproof shield, it had stopped whatever I crashed into when the plane hit the trees. I would never know for sure, but I was glad I had it. The best thing that ever happened to me was that my skateboard didn't fit in the overhead bin.

I had no idea how long I had been laying there. It could have been seconds after the crash, or I could have slept a whole night. It was daytime, in any case. When I rolled over and saw the front of the plane about twenty yards to the left of me, I felt sore all over. Every muscle ached. Most likely I had tensed up just before we hit the trees. That's what happened. I remember somebody once told me that drunks often survive car crashes because they're so out of it they don't tense up their muscles. When you tense your muscles, you get hurt.

I felt my arms and legs. Nothing was broken, as far as I could tell. There were cuts on my arms and some blood, but nothing too serious.

My shoulders were bruised. My head was throbbing with pain. But I could stand. I could move all my limbs. I could see, hear, and smell.

Hey, I was alive. That was what mattered. I had survived. Anything was better than the alternative.

The first thing I thought of was that book, *Hatchet*, my sister had been reading. I had to read it in fourth grade. The kid was in one of those little two-seater prop planes when the pilot had a heart attack. The plane crash-landed in the wilderness and all the kid had was a hatchet. He used it to build a shelter, make a fire, kill an animal, everything. Julia loved that book. I think she read it four or five times.

Julia! Suddenly, I remembered my sister, and Henry and David, and all those old ladies. They must still be in the plane!

Thoughts raced through my brain. What if I was the only survivor? My parents made me promise to keep an eye on Julia, and now she was dead. My best friends were dead. *Everybody* was dead except me. Was it my fault? What right did I have to be alive while they were all dead?

But wait! Maybe the others weren't dead. Maybe they were still in the plane. Maybe . . .

I struggled to my feet and ran toward the plane. Or what was left of the plane, anyway. Only the front section was still there. It was obvious what had happened. The nose had come down between the trunks of two trees. They must have ripped off the wings on each side and taken the rear of the plane with them. The front separated from the rest of the plane like a rocket separates in stages. It skidded along the ground until it was stopped by a tree. The nose was touching the base of the tree. I couldn't even see where the rest of the plane was. Maybe it blew up.

The cockpit windshield was shattered. There were little pieces of glass scattered around on the ground. I must have gone flying through the windshield when we hit the tree and landed on the ground outside the plane.

"Julia!" I hollered. "Henry! David!"

No answer. The cockpit window was too high off the ground to climb into. So I ran to the tree. There was a low branch I could grab and pull myself up on. My arms and legs were sore, but I did it. From the first branch, I grabbed another branch and shimmied along it until I could reach the window. I didn't think about my pain. I was thinking about my sister and my friends.

I pulled myself up until I could see inside the cockpit. There were bodies in there. They were on the floor, tangled up in a crazy mess of arms and legs. There was moaning. *Somebody* was alive. I struggled to climb in through the hole where the window used to be. Some of the glass still had to be knocked away.

"Julia!" I yelled, grabbing my sister and shaking her. "Come on, get up!"

"Stop it," she moaned. "My leg is killing me. I think it's broken."

I was so happy she was alive, I didn't care if every bone in her body was broken.

"I'm okay," Henry said, rolling over on his back. "I'll help Squirt. You see about David."

"I'm fine," David said, coughing and struggling to his feet. "It's *her* I'm worried about."

The flight attendant, Arcadia, was still on the floor, lying on her side with her eyes closed.

"Is she alive?" I asked.

David knelt down and put his ear to Arcadia's face.

"She's breathing, I think," he said.

"It's going to be hard to carry her and Julia out through the window," I said.

Henry and David looked at me like I was stupid.

"You climbed in through the window?" David asked.

"Well, yeah," I said. "How else do you think I got in here?"

They both looked toward the rear of the plane. Or I should say, where the rear of the plane *used* to be. Everything behind the first class section was gone. There was just a big hole there. I didn't have to climb in the window. I could have simply walked right into the plane from the hole in the back. It hadn't even occurred to me. I must have been in shock.

"Here, grab her legs," David told me.

David and I carried Arcadia out the back and lowered her gently on the ground. She didn't open her eyes. She was asleep, or maybe unconscious. Henry carried Julia out of the plane. We gathered around Arcadia.

"What do you think we should do?" I asked.

"I don't see any bleeding," Henry said. "She could be in shock."

"We should wake her up," Julia said. "She could lapse into a coma."

"Anybody know how to do CPR?" I asked.

"Is that the same as mouth-to-mouth resuscitation?" Henry asked.

"I do!" David quickly volunteered.

I had to laugh. It felt *good* to laugh. Despite everything that had happened, despite the fact that our plane had been hijacked and we had to kill some guys and we almost died in the crash, I had to laugh. There was a smile on Henry's face too.

"Hey, I want to give her mouth-to-mouth resuscitation!" Henry said. "I took a course in CPR once."

"You took a course in *everything* once," I said. "I talked to her first. I should be the one who gets to give her mouth-to-mouth resuscitation."

"I called it!" David said. "I got dibs."

"You guys are sick," Julia told us.

"Hey, it's not that different from kissing," insisted Henry.

"I'm *fine*," Arcadia said, sitting up suddenly. She scared the carp out of us.

"Oh," me and David and Henry said, only partly relieved that Arcadia was okay. None of us would need to give her mouth-to-mouth resuscitation. Briefly, I allowed myself to think about how nice it might be to pass out and have Arcadia give *me* mouth-to-mouth resuscitation.

"What happened?" Arcadia asked, struggling to her feet.

"Henry is the hero," I explained. "He steered the front of the plane between two trees. That sheared off the wings and the rest of the plane. You can't even see it from here. We must have skidded on the ground a long way. I went flying through the windshield. We carried you out."

"It was luck," Henry said. "A miracle, really."

"Are you guys okay?" Arcadia asked.

"Yeah, mostly," Henry said. "I think Squirt's leg is broken."

"I'll be fine," my sister said, but she was wincing with pain.

"I can make a splint for her," Arcadia said. "We need to stabilize the injured area. We're trained for this kind of thing. What about all the other passengers? Those old ladies?"

"We don't know," David said. "Dead, I guess."

I felt guilty about laughing and fantasizing about kissing Arcadia. People had died. Not just the hijackers, who deserved it. But those nice old ladies, those old ladies with their blue hair. They never hurt anybody. All they wanted to do was go to their knitting convention. And now they were dead.

Arcadia started crying first. Then it was this

contagious thing like when one person yawns and then the person next to them yawns. I started crying too. I guess Henry figured that if I was crying it was okay for him to cry and he also started crying. Then Julia started crying and even David, who I don't think *ever* cried in his life, started crying. None of us even knew any of those old ladies, but all five of us were sobbing and we couldn't stop. And why not? Even though we were probably the luckiest people in the world, we had just been through the most horrible experience of our lives. We had to do something, and crying seemed to make more sense than laughing. I couldn't imagine that I would ever have a reason to laugh again.

"What are all you babies bawling about?" somebody said.

We turned around to see who it was.

Mildred Herschel was standing there.

CHAPTER 8:
The Luckiest Unlucky People

"It looks like I'm going to be late for my knitting convention," Mrs. Herschel said, brushing some dirt off her dress. "Blast it!"

"Mrs. Herschel!" I shouted.

She was messed up pretty good, like all of us. Her dress was torn and her gray hair wasn't neatly in place, the way it had been when we took off. Her glasses were broken. There was a dark smudge on her face. But she was alive, and Arcadia went over to hug her.

"How did you get here?" David asked. "You were in the back of the plane."

"Everything from the wings on back got

stuck between two trees," she said. "I'm a lucky bugger. I had my seat belt off. The impact threw me clear of the wreckage. I figured the front of the plane must have broken off and slid forward. Had to walk a kilometer or so until I found you."

"What about the others?" Arcadia asked. "Your friends?"

"I don't know," Mrs. Herschel said softly, "I didn't look back." And then she began to tear up quietly and put her head on Arcadia's shoulder.

So it looked like there were six of us who made it out alive. Me and my sister. Henry and David. Mrs. Herschel and Arcadia. We were all banged up, but the worst injury was Julia's leg. We were probably the luckiest unlucky people in the world.

Henry went back in the plane to see what we had that might be useful. There was a first-aid kit, a defibrillator, a life raft, and a fire extinguisher. He couldn't find the axe that the hijacker had been waving around at us.

Arcadia went to a nearby tree and ripped off a few straight branches and some vines.

"Sit down," she told Julia. "You need to keep that leg out straight so it'll heal right."

Arcadia seemed to know what she was talking about. Julia's leg was swollen, painful, and she couldn't put weight on it, which meant it was probably broken. Arcadia said that maybe it was just a hairline fracture. She started working on her splint. Henry and I ripped another branch off and made it into a simple crutch for Julia.

I knew there was a lot we had to do. We should probably be getting some water and food, maybe building a shelter. But I was just so tired. The sun was lower in the sky and it would be dark out soon. It had been a long day. No point in trying to get anything done. I flopped down on the ground and sat back-to-back against my sister to give each of us something to lean on. At home, we would do that sometimes and see if we could stand up without using our hands.

I guess the others were as exhausted as I was. They formed a little circle on the ground, while Arcadia worked on Julia's leg.

As I looked around, I was grateful for one thing. At least we were a group. What if I had been the only survivor? I don't know if I could handle it, being out there all alone in the woods at night. I would have freaked out.

We were all tired, but it was the kind of tired where you're so tired that you can't sleep. We were all revved up over what had happened to us. We had seen death close up. It was still sinking in. You can't just roll over and fall asleep after that.

Mrs. Herschel told us she was going to turn eighty years old in a few days. She had been planning to celebrate in California with her children and grandchildren. She said she used to be a champion roller skater "in her day." I couldn't imagine her on skates.

Arcadia told us she came from New Orleans. She said she became a flight attendant right after high school so she would get to see the world.

"From the time I was a little girl, I always loved to fly," she said, shaking her head.

It got quiet. We were all lost in our own thoughts. I shivered. I didn't know if it was because it was a little cold out, or because of what we had been through. I had never been close to death before.

There was sound in the distance. Some kind of an animal, maybe.

"You think there are wolves out here?" Henry asked in a hushed tone. "Squirt can't run. She'd be a sitting duck if we were attacked."

"Wolves are afraid of people," Julia said. "They'd run from *us*."

It got quiet again. All I could hear were the leaves rustling in the trees. It was getting dark.

"I'll say one thing," Arcadia said. "I'll never complain about anything ever again. I don't care what happens to me. I'm just grateful to be alive."

"Thank God," said David.

"What do you think happened to *them*?" Arcadia asked.

"Them?" I said.

"Those guys. The ones who hijacked the plane."

"I know one thing," David said. "They didn't go to heaven."

"That's where they were *trying* to go," Henry said. "Did you hear that guy yelling during the fight? He said he welcomed death and that they'd all meet in heaven."

I remembered. Just before Henry nailed him with the fire extinguisher, the guy screamed, "Eternal bliss will be ours!" I'll never forget it.

"Guys like that go to hell," David stated firmly. "That's all there is to it."

"How do you know?" Henry asked quietly.

"Thou shalt not kill," David said. "It's right there in the Bible."

"The hijackers believed in some kind of a Bible, or holy book too," Henry said. "They believed in a god. They thought they were doing God's will. What makes you so sure your god is right and theirs is wrong?"

"Because I'm sitting here and they're dead, that's how," David said. "What's the matter? Don't you believe in God? Why do you think we're alive?"

"Because we got lucky," Henry said. "You think God loves us more than all those people who died? Where was God when that guy killed the flight attendant?"

Wow. I never heard anyone suggest they didn't believe in God before. Julia and I had gone to Hebrew school, and I had my bar mitzvah. I knew that David went to church every Sunday and Henry didn't, but that was as far as it went. The three of us guys had never had a discussion about religion before. Mostly, we talked about skateboarding. To be honest, I had never given much thought to religion before. I guess I just believed what I was told.

"So you're an atheist," David said to Henry. "Why don't you believe in God?"

"Why should I?" Henry replied. "It's not like God is sitting here talking with us and I'm pretending I don't see him. Where is he? Where was he on 9/11? Where is he whenever there's a natural disaster? Where is he whenever *anything* bad happens?"

"God isn't like some superhero who flies in to save the day," Arcadia said. "Whatever happens, good or bad, is all part of his plan."

"So his plan was for those old ladies to die?" Henry asked. "Some plan."

"I believe God chose us to be on that plane," David said. "He knew we were strong, that we would know what to do. God plans everything."

"Then you have to believe God planned the hijacking, too," Henry said. "If you're gonna give him credit for the good things, you have to blame him for the bad stuff, too. So when babies die, and kids starve, and people get run over by drunk drivers, God planned all that stuff. Right?"

Wow. I never heard anybody say anything like that before. Certainly not Henry. He was never serious. Most of the time he was the one who kept us laughing.

"Forgive him for what he says," David said, putting his hands together.

"And why would he let me survive, the atheist?" Henry continued. "There are a lot of dead believers back there."

"God works in mysterious ways," David explained. "On Judgment Day, we'll understand."

"I'll tell you what I think," Henry said. "I think we all become worm food when we die."

"I believe in God," said Arcadia.

"I don't know what I believe," said Julia.

I looked over at Mrs. Herschel. She was being quiet. I guess I figured that somebody her age must know something the rest of us didn't. She must have gained some wisdom in all those years.

"I don't know if there is a God, or an afterlife, or whatever," she said. "There's no way any of us can know. Anybody who claims they know is a liar or a fake. But I'll tell you one thing. I'll find out before any of you."

It got quiet again.

"We'd better get some rest," Arcadia finally said.

She finished wrapping the vines around Julia's leg to hold the splint in place. Then she cleared a little spot on the ground and tried to make herself comfortable.

"G'night, y'all," she said, closing her eyes.

It was dark now and almost impossible to see. I found a smooth spot to lay down on. If the wolves or mountain lions were going to come and eat me, I guess there was nothing I could do about it. The others lay down too and said good night. Somebody was sobbing quietly. I couldn't tell who it was.

I wasn't going to cry. Whether it was God's will or random chance, the six of us had survived. In all probability, somebody would be there to rescue us by the time we woke up in the morning. Life would return to normal.

CHAPTER 9:
The Least We Could Do

I couldn't sleep. The ground was hard. The noises were creepy. We had been through a lot. There were bugs crawling on me.

Maybe I dozed off a little at some point. When I woke up, I didn't open my eyes right away. I wanted to remember the incredible dream I'd had. I was in a plane crash with my sister and two of my friends. We survived, and so did this old lady and a really cute flight attendant. Great dream. It felt so real.

Soon I'd wake up, go downstairs to get a glass of orange juice and say hi to my mom and dad. Maybe one of them would be able to give me a ride to the skatepark at the mall if they didn't have too many errands to run. If not, I'd just get together with the guys and we'd skate the ledges over by the middle school.

I was lost in these thoughts when a squirrel jumped over my legs. I screamed. This was not my bedroom. I wouldn't be going skating today. I was in the woods. It wasn't a dream.

There was no sound of helicopters waiting to take us home. There were no friendly rescuers with food and water and clean clothes for us. No news media to interview us about the ordeal we had been through. There were just the six of us lying in the dirt in the middle of the forest. David was already awake, fussing off to the side of our little campsite with some sticks. The others were opening their eyes and stretching, probably only awake because I screamed. Julia got up and hobbled around despite the splint on her leg.

"Zimmerman, you scared him away!" David complained. "I was gonna eat that squirrel for breakfast."

"What are you doing?" I asked David.

"I call it the Deathtrap," he said. "I dug this hole in the ground and covered it with leaves. If an animal runs over the leaves he falls in. There are even sharp sticks at the bottom to stab him."

"That's lovely," I said. The thought of killing and eating a squirrel for breakfast made me feel sick to my stomach.

"Any sign of a plane or rescue team?" asked Arcadia as she got up and brushed the dust and twigs from her flight attendant's uniform.

"No," David said, "and I've been up for over an hour. Arcadia, grab some of those branches from that tree, will you? We need to build some kind of a shelter. Henry, maybe you can see if there's a brook or stream or source of water nearby. And Julia, why don't you and Jimmy look around for nuts or something we can eat? We've got a lot to do. Am I the only one who's starved?"

"What shall I do?" Mrs. Herschel asked. "Would you like me to make a rocking chair out of sticks and sit in it?"

David stopped fussing with the branches and stared at Mrs. Herschel, as if he wasn't sure if she was goofing on him or not.

"You can—" David started.

"Don't you tell *me* what I should do!" Mrs. Herschel scolded. "Who made you king of the forest? Why don't you sit down and put a sock in it?"

Whoa! David sat down right where he was, almost falling into his Deathtrap. He does have a tendency to boss people around. There have been more than a few times when Henry and I got into arguments with David and he walked out on us when he didn't get his way. But he always comes back. I was glad that David took charge when we were on the plane. I guess he decided that one of us had to be the leader on the ground too, and it should be him.

"Sonny," Mrs. Herschel continued. "I grew up during the 1930s. We had the Depression in England too. I worked in a factory putting together airplanes during World War II. I lived through Hitler and the Nazis and the Cold War. What have you done in your bleeding life? Roll down the street on a piece of wood with wheels on it?"

"Hey, no problem," David said. "You can be in charge if you want."

"I don't want to be in charge!" Mrs. Herschel replied. "But a kilometer away are a bunch of my closest friends. I think that before we fuss with eating and drinking and building shelters, we should give them a proper burial. You show respect for the dead. That's the least we can do for them."

"She's right," Arcadia said.

It was a long walk through the woods to find the rest of the plane. I told my sister to sit and rest her leg, but she insisted on coming with us. There were skid marks on the ground showing where our section of the plane had slid. It was amazing to think that we could slide so far through the woods.

Finally, we reached the back part of the plane. Or what was left of it, anyway. My guess had been right. The force of hitting two thick trees must have caused the front part of the plane to break off and slide forward. That's what saved our lives.

Even though we had run out of fuel, there must have been enough left in the wings to ignite the back of the plane. We were lucky it didn't burn down the whole forest. The metal frame was twisted and blackened. It was a miracle that Mrs. Herschel got out before the fire destroyed the back of the plane.

Unfortunately, there weren't any people left for us to find. We looked all over for survivors. None of us said a word until we were finished combing the area. A few of us stopped in the middle to go off to the side and cry, be sick, whatever.

"I hope your friends didn't suffer much," Arcadia said, putting an arm around Mrs. Herschel.

David found a piece of metal from the plane that was shaped a little bit like a cross. He stuck it in the ground and said a prayer. We were all shaken. Even Henry bowed his head. I'll never think of people the same way again.

We searched for any food, water, or supplies that we could salvage from the wreck, but there was nothing. Everything had burned. Scattered behind the plane were some suitcases that must have fallen out of the cargo hold before the plane exploded.

"Would it be disrespectful for us to take this luggage?" I asked Mrs. Herschel. "There might be something inside we can use."

"I'm sure my friends would be honored if we made use of anything they had," she replied.

"We'll need to make a few trips to carry it all," Julia said.

"No," replied Mrs. Herschel. "Let's take everything now. I don't want to come back here ever again."

Each of us grabbed a couple of suitcases and lugged them back to the campsite with us.

CHAPTER 10:
Priorities

The suitcases were *heavy*. What do old ladies bring with them when they go to conventions, I wondered. Weights? When we finally made it back to our campsite, Mrs. Herschel suggested we open the suitcases right away. She thought there might be food or water in there that could hold us over until we got rescued.

There wasn't. Mostly, the suitcases were filled with clothing—those funny-looking patterned dresses that old ladies wear all the time. We took out some nail clippers that might come in handy down the line, but we didn't have much use for cotton balls, soap, cameras, dental floss, or jars of Vaseline. Our hopes soared when Julia found a cell phone, but it wouldn't get a signal. None of our cell phones worked. That confirmed our suspicion that we were out of the United States. We were probably in Canada.

It felt strange, going through the luggage of a person who was no longer alive. It felt like an invasion of their privacy. But we had to do it. There was always the chance that we might find something that would keep *us* alive.

"Hey, check it out!" Henry shouted as he went through one of the pocketbooks. "Jackpot!"

Henry held up a hundred-dollar bill.

"We're rich!" said Julia.

"There are ten of them in here," Henry said. "A thousand bucks."

"A lot of good that'll do us," said Arcadia. "I'd rather find a cell phone that works."

Mrs. Herschel looked at the name tag attached to the suitcase that had money in it. It said "Ann Constantine" on it.

"Annie was planning to spend a few days in Las Vegas after the convention was over," she said sadly. "She loved playing those beastly slot machines."

Henry gave Mrs. Herschel the money to hold and repacked the bag neatly. We put the suitcases in a pile under a big piece of metal so they wouldn't get wet. That's when I noticed David was chewing something.

Maybe it was a leaf, I figured. But then he slipped his hand in his pocket, took something out, and put it in his mouth. I wasn't the only one who noticed.

"Hey, put that down!" Arcadia told him. Everybody looked at David.

"What are you eating?" Julia asked him.

"Pretzels," he admitted. "They were in one

of the suitcases. What's the big deal?"

"If it's no big deal, why were you hiding them?" demanded Arcadia.

"I wasn't hiding them!" David insisted.

"There are six of us here!" Mrs. Herschel said to him. "We're *all* hungry! What makes you decide that *you* should get the only food we have?"

"Man!" David said. "You people need to lighten up. We're not stranded on some desert island. Lots of people are looking for us. We'll probably be rescued any minute. Here, take the stupid bag of pretzels if you want 'em so badly."

He flipped the bag to Arcadia, but she dropped it. A few of the pretzels fell in the dirt. Ordinarily, any of us would have thrown them away. Arcadia scooped the loose pretzels up and put them back in the bag.

"Are you daft?" Mrs. Herschel said to David. "What if we're *not* rescued right away? What if it takes weeks for anyone to find us? What if it takes months? You don't know what's going to happen. We might need these pretzels to save one of us who is dying from starvation."

"Not cool, Dave," Henry said.

None of us had much to say after that, and we puttered around trying to look busy, but mostly trying not to look at each other.

"What's *taking* them so long?" Arcadia finally said, peering up through the trees.

"Yeah, it's been about twenty-four hours since the crash," Henry said.

"It could be longer than that," Julia pointed out. "We might have been unconscious for a while."

"They should have found us by now," Arcadia said.

They were right. The sky was blue. Not a cloud up there. There was no reason why we couldn't have been rescued.

"We might have flown way off course," I guessed. "That's probably why they're having trouble finding us."

"Are you kidding me?" David asked. "This is the twenty-first century. They've got GPS, emergency-locator transmitters, position-indicating radio beacons. They've got satellites with cameras that are so powerful they can read license plates from outer space. They've got night-vision goggles. Search and rescue teams with 4 x 4s, dogs, ground trackers, and guys on horseback. They can find anybody if they want to."

"Every plane has a black box," Arcadia said. "It would tell exactly where the plane is, and the box is so strong it can survive any crash."

"I saw this comedian on TV once," Henry said. "He said that if the metal they use to make those black boxes is so strong, why don't they just make planes out of them?"

Nobody was in the mood to laugh. Henry only made things worse by explaining that if a plane was made of really strong stuff, it wouldn't crash. Nothing kills a joke more than explaining it.

"Under the circumstances, I don't find that very amusing," Mrs. Herschel said.

"Y'know, maybe the roads around here are so bad, they just can't get to the crash site," I said. "Did you ever think of that?"

"Maybe we should go look for help," Henry suggested. "If they don't come to us, we should go to them. Who knows, maybe there's a gas station a few miles up the road."

"Road? What are you guys talking about?" David said. "There aren't any roads around here! We're in the middle of a forest. There might be not be a gas station for a hundred miles."

"Well, we may be here for a while," Mrs. Herschel said. "We might as well get used to it."

"I say we set our priorities," David said. "There are three basic human needs to survive, right? Food, water, and shelter. First, we should look for food. I'm starved."

"May I make a suggestion?"

We all looked at my sister. Julia had been mostly quiet during this discussion. She's a very smart kid, but she tries not to show it when she's around people who are older than she is. She kind of lies back and keeps her mouth shut.

"Go for it, Squirt," Henry said.

"I was thinking that maybe our first priority should be to make a fire."

David busted out laughing.

"No offense, Squirt, but that's probably the dumbest idea I ever heard," he told my sister. "What do we need a fire for? We've got nothing to cook. It's not cold out, so we don't need the warmth. It's not nighttime, so we don't need the light. What do you want to do, sing campfire songs and make s'mores? If you ask me, we should be out hunting for food right now before we starve to death. *That* should be the priority."

"But if we had a fire—," Julia began.

"Besides," David interrupted, "we don't have matches or lighters or anything."

Julia didn't argue. She's not the confrontational type. She just shrugged and put up her hands.

"It was just an idea," she said.

At that moment, I heard something in the distance. I couldn't place the sound at first, but after a few seconds, it got louder and more obvious—it was a *plane*! They were coming for us! We were going to be rescued!

Looking up through the trees, I could see it. It was one of those little single engine Cessnas. Everybody realized what it was at the same moment.

Well, you never heard such yelling and

screaming. We were all jumping up and down and waving our arms. I picked a piece of the plane's windshield off the ground and tried to catch a ray of sunlight and reflect it toward the sky.

Nothing was happening. I kept looking for the plane to turn around or wiggle its wings, maybe shoot off a flare or something to let us know they'd seen us. But it just kept going in a straight line. We were still shouting, but no longer jumping.

"How can they not see our plane?" Henry said.

"It's on the floor of the forest," Mrs. Herschel said. "They can't see it through the treetops."

I tracked the Cessna a few more seconds until it passed behind the trees and out of my field of view.

"Where is it?" Henry yelled.

The engine sound got quieter and quieter until we couldn't hear it. Nobody was shouting anymore. The plane was gone.

One by one, we all looked at Julia.

"*That's* why we need a fire," she said.

CHAPTER 11:
Fire

A fire. Of course! Fire not only cooks food, warms you up, and creates light, it can also be a distress signal. If we had a fire, it would have produced smoke and that plane would have seen it. We would have been rescued. It was so obvious now. My little sister was the only one who realized it.

"How are we going to make a bloody fire?" Mrs. Herschel asked.

I looked at Julia. She probably has every ribbon, badge, and award the Girl Scouts give out. She *must* know all about fires. But she kept her mouth shut.

"Did anyone come across a book of matches in the suitcases?" Arcadia asked. "A lighter?"

Everybody shook their heads.

"This is one situation where *not* smoking can be hazardous to your health," Henry said.

"I know how to start a fire," David said.

David had kept his mouth shut ever since the plane flew overhead. He knew he'd made an idiot of himself saying we didn't need a fire, and must have been working very hard to keep quiet. But David is just not the kind of person who can sit back and let other people take charge.

"I saw this in a movie once," he said. "Somebody get me a smooth, straight stick, about a foot and a half long."

David had us run around the woods to get him all the stuff he needed—firewood, a little chunk of wood, a bigger piece he could use as a base, and a shoelace, which Henry contributed.

David peeled the smooth stick until it had a point at one end. Then he wrapped the shoelace around the middle of that stick once, and put it pointy end down against the base. He had me hold the wood chunk against the top of the stick to press it down against the base.

"When I pull on each end of the shoelace," he said as he demonstrated, "it spins the stick. See? That creates friction. Friction makes heat. Heat produces sparks. Sparks give us fire."

It made sense, I suppose. I pushed the block down on top of the stick and David began pulling on the two ends of the shoelace one at a time to spin the stick. It was a pretty ingenious little machine, I had to admit.

The only problem was, it didn't make any heat, sparks, or fire. After five minutes of furious spinning, the point of the stick was barely warm. At this rate, it might take a week to make a spark.

"What was the name of that movie you saw this in?" I asked.

David ignored the remark and went back to work, pulling the shoelace back and forth even faster. I could see the sweat beading up on his forehead. He stopped, panting.

"Wow, that's some inferno," Henry said. "We might have to call the fire department to put out the blaze."

"How about *you* take over for a while?" David suggested to Henry. "My arms are tired."

"I'm tired just from *watching* you do that," Henry said.

I sure didn't want to do it. The girls weren't volunteering either.

"You got a better idea?" David asked.

"It's not gonna work, David," I told him. I have to admit that in some weird way, I was happy to see him fail.

"It will *too* work!" David insisted. "You've got to be patient, Zimmerman!"

"Can I try?" Julia asked timidly.

"Knock yourself out, Squirt," David said, handing her the stick and shoelace.

"Thanks," Julia said, "but I'd like to try something else."

Julia hobbled over to the suitcases we had found near the back of the plane. She opened one up and came back with a bag of cotton balls and a jar of Vaseline.

"What are you gonna do, Squirt?" David asked. "Put on your makeup?"

Julia ripped open the bag and took out a few cotton balls. Then she opened the Vaseline and smeared some on a cotton ball. I had no idea what she was trying to accomplish.

She asked me to take the sticks we had gathered and separate them into four piles: skinny sticks, *really* skinny sticks, fat sticks, and fatter sticks. She picked up a few of the skinniest sticks and broke them into tiny pieces. Then she mashed them into the cotton ball.

"We could really use some paper," she said.

"Where are we gonna get paper?" David said.

"Oh, I have some," said Mrs. Herschel. She reached into her pocket and took out those hundred dollar bills.

"You're going to use *bills* to get the fire started?" Arcadia asked.

"The money won't do Annie any good," Mrs. Herschel said. "I don't think you can change a hundred in heaven."

"Rip it into the thinnest strips you possibly can," Julia told Mrs. Herschel.

"That's a hundred bucks!" David said as Mrs. Herschel tore the bill down the middle. "What if we can't get a fire going?"

"Then I wasted a hundred dollars," Julia admitted.

Mrs. Herschel gave each of us a hundred-dollar bill and we shredded them into tiny strips. Julia mashed the strips up into a big, fluffy ball the same way you would make a snowball. Then she pushed one of the Vaseline-covered cotton balls partly into it.

"This has got to rank up there with the dumbest things I've ever seen," David said. "That's six hundred bucks you just tore up."

"It's a fireball," Julia explained. "Vaseline is petroleum jelly. Petroleum burns."

"But how are you going to light it?" Arcadia asked.

"Does anybody have a magnifying glass?" Julia asked.

"Of *course* we don't have a magnifying glass!" David said. "Why didn't you think of that before you ripped up the six hundred bucks?"

"Oh, get stuffed," Mrs. Herschel told him. "It's not your money."

"Any glass might do," Julia said. "Do we have a bottle? Binoculars? A piece of the windshield might even work."

"My friend, Agnes, loved taking pictures," Mrs. Herschel said excitedly. "I'm pretty sure she had a camera in her suitcase."

"Can you look, please?" Julia said.

Mrs. Herschel went through the suitcases until she found her friend's camera. It was a nice one, not one of those junky little disposables or a PHD camera (push here, dummy).

"Would it be it okay to take it apart?" Julia asked. "We only need the lens."

Mrs. Herschel tried to pull the lens off, but it wouldn't unscrew. She looked at the camera for a moment, and I thought she was going to hand it to one of us, but she didn't. Instead, she raised the camera up over her head and smashed it against a rock. It broke into a few pieces and the lens fell off.

"Agnes won't mind," said Mrs. Herschel.

"Maybe it's still under warranty," Henry said.

Julia breathed on the lens and wiped it with her T-shirt. Then she looked up into the trees. It must have been around noon. We were in the shade, but I could tell the sun was high in the sky.

"Let's move over there," Julia said, pointing to a patch of sun between the trees about thirty feet away.

Each of us grabbed a pile of sticks. Julia carried the camera lens and her fireball. She sat down on a patch of dirt in the sun and put the fireball on the ground.

"A convex lens takes a beam of light and concentrates the rays on one spot," she said. "If you hold it at the right distance from an object, it generates a lot of heat."

"That's not gonna work," David said.

"Maybe not," Julia admitted.

She held the lens above the cotton ball. The circle of sunlight was about an inch wide, so Julia moved the lens closer. The circle got smaller, until it was a tiny white pinpoint.

"I used to do that with bugs in the field across from my house," Henry said. "But they never caught on fire."

"Burning bugs is sick," Arcadia said.

"*All* guys do that," I told her.

"All guys are sick," Arcadia said.

Suddenly, a tiny puff of smoke came off the cotton ball.

"It's working!" Mrs. Herschel said.

Julia held the lens steady and the smoke kept puffing up, but there was no flame.

"We need a spark," Henry said. "We need some friction."

Friction? I had an idea. I ran to get my skateboard.

"This may not be the best time for skating," Arcadia said when I got back.

"The grip tape on the top of the board feels a lot like that little black strip on a matchbook," I told them. "Maybe we can use it to make a spark."

"Genius runs in the family," Henry said.

There were plenty of sharp objects around. I grabbed a shard of metal and scraped it against the grip tape. Nothing. I tried throwing it at the grip tape. No sparks. A piece of glass from the windshield didn't do anything either. Maybe grip tape wouldn't work.

Henry picked up some rocks and rubbed each one against the grip tape. The first few didn't do anything, but the fourth one made a tiny spark.

"Bring it over here!" Julia said excitedly.

Henry held the skateboard right next to the fireball and scraped the rock back and forth against the grip tape. Julia kept the beam of light focused on the spot and leaned over and blew gently on the fireball. The little plume of smoke kept puffing away. Then, somehow, Henry managed to shoot one of the sparks on the spot where Julia was focusing the sunlight.

A flame leaped to life.

CHAPTER 12:
Democracy in Action

"Fire! We have fire!"

It was so cool! The Vaseline ignited. That set the cotton ball on fire, which set the shredded money on fire, which set the little twigs on fire. It was beautiful.

Mrs. Herschel and Arcadia started dancing around like a couple of cavewomen who had discovered the secret of fire. Henry and I jumped up to join them.

Julia didn't join in the fun. She grabbed more skinny sticks and made a little tepee over the flame. When that caught fire, she took some of the thicker sticks and crisscrossed them on top. Then she took the biggest sticks and put them on. With each layer of sticks, the fire grew bigger.

"We have to make sure to leave a little room for air to get in," Julia said as she added wood to the fire and poked a stick into it to arrange it the way she wanted.

"Julia, you are The Man!" I said, so proud of my little sister. Everybody except David clapped her on the back.

The smoke rising off the fire wasn't all that visible as it snaked up through the trees. It didn't look like anyone would be able to see the signal. But Julia said we would build the fire bigger and that if another plane came by, we could throw some green leaves on the blaze to make the smoke darker. Until then, we had a nice little fire going that we could use for cooking, heat, light, and to keep bugs or animals away.

For the time being, there was something

comforting about just staring into it. I always loved staring at a fire.

"I wish we had marshmallows," Henry said, "and some hamburgers and hot dogs."

I had been feeling hungry for a while, but it wasn't until Henry said the word "hamburger" that I started to get that feeling in my stomach. It wanted to be filled. A hamburger would taste *so* good.

I tried to figure out how long it had been since my last meal. A day, at least. And that was just a bowl of corn flakes. I wished I had stuffed myself with food back then.

Maybe it would be better not to think about it, I decided. Just think about something else.

"Now that we've got a fire," David said, "we have to get something to cook. Something to eat."

"What are you going to do," Arcadia asked. "Catch a bear?"

I shivered, imagining in my head a bear

chasing us around and devouring us one at a time. What if there *were* bears in these woods? Or something more dangerous?

"Maybe we should sit down as a group and figure out what to do next," Henry suggested.

Sounded like a good idea. David snorted and rolled his eyes.

"Do we have to debate *everything*?" he asked. "Next you'll be telling me we need a Congress and a House of Representatives. You know, sometimes you just have to *act* and not sit around deciding what to do next. We waste so much time. It would be so much faster if one person made a decision."

"So you'd prefer a totalitarian form of government?" Mrs. Herschel asked.

"*Yes!*" David said. "We're hungry! Let's go get some food! End of debate. What's to discuss? What could make more sense? What's wrong with you people?"

"Y'know, you don't know everything,"

Arcadia said to David. "You were wrong when you said we didn't need a fire. You were wrong when you tried to make the fire too."

"Was I wrong about going after those hijackers?" David asked. "Lucky we didn't have to vote on *that*, huh? If I hadn't done anything, we'd all be dead now."

He was right, I had to admit.

"I have an idea!" Henry piped up. "Let's vote on it!"

"Vote on what?" I asked.

"Let's vote on whether or not we should vote on stuff."

I wasn't sure if Henry was kidding or not.

"That's stupid," David said.

"All in favor of voting on stuff raise your hand," Henry said, sticking his hand in the air.

Mrs. Herschel put her hand up right away. Then Arcadia raised her hand. So did Julia. I put my hand up too.

"All opposed to voting on stuff raise your hand," Henry said.

"You expect me to vote against voting?" David asked.

"It doesn't matter whether or not you vote," Arcadia said. "We already have a majority."

David stood up abruptly and started marching around, like he was really mad.

"Do you guys remember why we started the Woodpushers?" he asked. "We didn't like rules. We didn't want to play football or soccer or basketball with their rules and clocks and uniforms. We didn't want to be on a team. We wanted to do our own thing. Remember?"

"We're not skateboarding here," I reminded him. "This isn't a sport. We're trying to get along. And survive."

"We are a group," Mrs. Herschel said. "It will certainly be better for all of us if we can find a way to work together instead of separately."

"Well, I'll tell you what," David said. "I say it's every man for himself. You folks can sit around gabbing and voting until you all starve to death. I'm going to get something to eat. See you later."

"Fine," Arcadia said. "Have fun."

David took a few steps, and then turned around and stopped.

"Hey, Zimmerman," he said, "can I borrow your board?"

"What for?" I asked.

"Maybe there's a halfpipe in the middle of the forest," David said.

I laughed and handed him my board. The nearest flat surface was probably a hundred miles away. David took the board and headed out into the woods.

"We shouldn't let him leave," Mrs. Herschel said.

"I'd like to see you stop him," muttered Henry.

"Good riddance, I say," Arcadia said once David was out of earshot. "How do you deal with that guy?"

"He'll be back," I said. "He always comes back."

CHAPTER 13:
Water

As soon as David left, I felt better. We all did, I think. It was like a big sigh of relief. That's the way he is. I love the guy like a brother and all, but he just gets on your nerves sometimes.

I wondered who would be our leader now. Not me. I didn't want the responsibility. Julia's not the leader type. Henry pretty much just likes to sit back and make fun of the world. I didn't know Arcadia or Mrs. Herschel very well, but neither of them seemed like a real take-charge kind of person the way David is. Mrs. Herschel was certainly the oldest in our group, so I guess she felt she had to start things off.

"Okay, our first order of business—"

"Um, may I say something?" Arcadia asked.

"Of course, dear," Mrs. Herschel said.

"I have to go to the bathroom," said Arcadia.

"So go," Julia said. "There are plenty of trees."

"Uh, that's not the problem," Arcadia said.

"Well, what's the problem, dear?" asked Mrs. Herschel.

"None of the trees . . . have toilet paper," Arcadia finally said.

The rest of us had a good snicker, and even Arcadia giggled a little.

"Use leaves," Julia said. "All of the trees have *them*."

"Leaves?" Arcadia asked, turning all red and squishing up her nose.

"Just *do* it, dear," Mrs. Herschel told her. "Don't be embarrassed. We're all friends here."

"Just make sure you don't use poison ivy,"

Julia suggested. "That could be . . . uncomfort-able."

We all groaned and Arcadia went off into the woods. I didn't laugh or make fun of her, because I knew that sooner or later we would all be doing the same thing.

We talked a little bit about what we should do next, but Julia felt we should wait for Arcadia. She came back in a few minutes, with a little smile on her face.

"Feel better, dear?" asked Mrs. Herschel.

"Much," Arcadia said.

"So . . . how did it go?" I asked. "With the leaves, I mean."

"Fine," Arcadia said.

"Did everything . . . come out all right?" Henry asked.

"I'd rather not discuss it," Arcadia said.

"Let's get down to business," Mrs. Herschel said. "Your friend David wasn't the only one who was hungry. I'm sure we all are. Do you think he was right? Should we go off and search for food?"

That sounded like a good idea to me. I figured we could hunt down some berries or nuts or something that might tide us over until we were rescued.

"I don't think so," my little sister said, and we all turned to look at her. Julia tends to fade into the background until she says something really smart that nobody else thought of.

"Why not, sweetie?" Mrs. Herschel asked. "Aren't you hungry too?"

"I learned in Girl Scouts that the average person can survive for more than a month without food," Julia said. "But we can't go more than a few days without water."

"Is that so?" Mrs. Herschel said.

"We're already dehydrated," Julia said. "Water accounts for almost two thirds of your body's weight. So I think it might be smarter to look for water before we worry about getting food."

I couldn't help but smile at my little sister. She was always the smart one in the family. I used to make fun of her because her head was always stuck in a book. But I guess she actually learned a thing or two.

"It sounds like the Girl Scouts taught you a great deal," Mrs. Herschel said, stroking Julia's hair. "Do you know anything about finding water?"

"A little," Julia said.

She was being modest. She knew a lot, about *everything*. The rest of us knew *one* way to get water—by turning on a faucet. So we were all ears.

"Let's go through those suitcases again," Julia said.

Julia told us to look for anything that could be used as a container. The cap from a can of shaving cream. A camera bag. An upside-down umbrella. We collected a bunch of containers. Julia said we should set them out in a clearing and use them to catch rain when it fell.

"Hey!" Henry said. "I found a bunch of plastic bags."

"Jackpot!" Julia said excitedly.

They were those really big black bags, the kind you use to line a garbage can. Julia ripped off a leafy bough from a bush and stuffed it into one of the bags. She sealed the opening with a rubber band she had in her pocket.

"What's that for?" Arcadia asked.

"It's called a solar still," Julia replied. "We'll leave it out in the sun. The moisture in the leaves won't be able to escape into the atmosphere, so it will collect in the bag. We should have a little water tomorrow."

My sister is a genius.

Julia said the solar still wouldn't produce

nearly enough water for all of us, so we'd have to go out and hunt for more. We were all a little nervous about leaving the safety of our little campsite, but it had to be done. Julia added some wood to the fire to keep it going while we were gone, and then she led the way. Julia grimaced as she limped along, putting her arm around my shoulder and using me like a crutch. It was slow going.

"Listen for a fast-moving stream," she advised us. "There might even be a river around here."

As we marched through the woods, I was looking all around me. There could be animals out there, I knew. But I was more worried about getting lost. What if we couldn't find our way back to the plane? What if a search and rescue team found the plane while we were gone? Well, at least they'd find our fire. They would know there were survivors somewhere.

I hadn't really been out in a forest since I was a little kid, when we used to go on family hikes. There were some woods near my house, but they cut them down and put up condos on that spot. Ever since then, my only experience with nature consisted of mowing the lawn.

Julia seemed to know where she was going, hobbling through the woods as if she'd been there a hundred times. The splint kept her bad leg straight, and she had picked up a long stick to use as a cane. Julia told us to keep an eye out for large rocks, which might have a big dent on top where water could collect.

We hiked around for a long time. I didn't tell the others, but I was starting to feel weak. It must have been even worse for Julia. Walking around looking for water uses up a lot of energy. And the more energy we used, the more water we'd need. I wondered if it might have made more sense to stay back at our campsite and wait for some rain or a rescue. Maybe we should have been conserving our energy. I stopped to wipe the sweat off my forehead when I turned my head and saw something through the trees.

A pond!

It was a sort of bowl in the ground where water collected. Not very big, maybe the size of a small house. But there was water in it. There was plenty for all of us.

"Water!" I shouted, pointing.

We went running over there like we were in the Olympics. Henry was the fastest, so he got to the edge of the pond first. He got down on his hands and knees and dipped his face into the water.

"Wait!" Julia yelled from behind us. "Don't drink it!"

Henry lifted his head out of the pond.

"Why not?" he asked, water dripping down his face.

"It's poisonous," Julia said as she limped over near the water.

"How do *you* know?" Arcadia asked.

"There's no vegetation around the pond," she replied. "The plants died."

"I've seen plenty of ponds that didn't have vegetation around them," Henry insisted. "This water looks fine to me."

But he didn't drink from it. We all watched as Julia walked around the pond for a minute. Then she kneeled down and picked something up.

"What's that?" Arcadia asked.

"A bone," Julia said. "It may be from a rabbit or a squirrel. Some small animal. I'm guessing it took its last drink here."

"But how could a pond out in the middle of nowhere get poisoned?" Mrs. Herschel asked. "It's not like there's a bloody toxic-waste dump around here."

Julia shrugged. "Who knows?" she said.

"Maybe some big animal happened to die around here and was lying in the water. I don't think it's safe to drink."

Oh, man! What a letdown. I could almost taste the water going down my throat. I could have gulped a gallon of it. A wave of depression swept over me. I think we all felt it. I *know* we all felt it, because Henry started crying. Mrs. Herschel and Arcadia went to comfort him, but he was beyond that.

"I just want a drink," he sobbed, "and something to eat."

"We'll dig a well if we have to," Julia told him. "We'll dig until we reach the water table."

"We'll find something to drink soon," I assured Henry. "I bet there's a water fountain right out here in the woods. Or maybe a soda machine. Did you bring any change with you?"

"It's not funny!" Henry shouted. "There's no water out here. We're gonna die in a few days!

We're finished! Nobody's gonna find us out here, Zimmerman! At some point, they'll give up trying! I should've gone with David. I'll bet *he* found water. I'll bet he found food."

I couldn't blame Henry for freaking out. We were all on edge. We had seen blood and death. We very nearly died ourselves. We were hot and sweaty, hungry and dehydrated. On top of all that, poor Henry had never even been away from home before. He wasn't about to say how much he missed his parents, but I knew he did because that's how I felt. I put my arm around him and held him while he cried.

That's when we heard a loud crack. It had to be one of three things.

Lightning.

A tree falling.

Or a gunshot.

CHAPTER 14:
What a Glorious Feeling

And then it started raining.

I hadn't noticed the clouds gathering over-head while we were searching for water. But the sky had darkened and when we looked up through the trees, storm clouds were sliding across the sky and lightning was flickering in the distance.

There was never a drizzle. Almost right away, the rain came down in sheets. We were under the trees, so it didn't hit us full force. But none of us needed to be told what to do. We ran out into the clearing and opened our mouths.

The rain tasted so good. It was like when

you're all sweaty on a really hot day and you've been skateboarding for hours and you take that first drink. But even better. The water was fresher, cooler. Or maybe it was just that my body needed it so badly.

"Drink up," Mrs. Herschel advised. "It could be a long time until we see rain again."

She didn't have to tell me. I filled myself with water. Henry cheered up almost instantly. After we drank as much as we could hold, Julia took out one of the plastic garbage bags and we held it wide open to catch some rain for later. We got a couple of gallons in there when Julia said we'd better tie the bag up or it would become too heavy and burst when we tried to carry it back to the campsite.

The rain was still pouring down and we were all drenched and laughing and happily dancing around. My sister just laughed. For all we knew, we were about to get hit by lightning, but it was a risk we were willing to take. And then something really weird happened.

Mrs. Herschel took off her clothes!

"What are you doing?" Arcadia shouted over the storm.

"What does it look like?" Mrs. Herschel said. "I'm taking a blooming shower!"

I couldn't believe it! I mean, I know we're born naked and all that. I know it's perfectly normal and natural to be nude. And when you think about it, wearing clothes is pretty abnormal, especially in the summer when it gets really hot. But here was this old lady peeling off her clothes like it was no big deal and dancing around in the rain! I didn't know if I should look at her, look away, or what. Mrs. Herschel even pulled a bar of soap out of the pocket of her dress and started soaping herself up with it. Who carries soap around with them?

"I'm taking a shower *too*!" Julia declared,

and she started peeling off her clothes.

"You are *not!*" I told her. I wasn't about to have my little sister parading around in the nude with all these people watching.

"Oh, lighten up, Jimmy!" Julia said.

There was nothing I could do. She had already pulled the splint off her leg, and then her pants were off, and they were so wet there was no way I was going to get them back on her.

"What a great idea!" Arcadia said, taking off her flight-attendant uniform. "Let's skinny-dip in the rain!"

I hadn't mentioned it to anybody, but before the rains came, we were all starting to smell pretty bad. Especially the guys. And with the dirt and the sweat and the stress and everything we had been through, a shower sounded really good. My clothes were smelly and ripped and soaked anyway.

But I wasn't sure I had the nerve to take my

clothes off. Mrs. Herschel and Arcadia were holding hands and dancing around. Julia was hopping around on one foot while she soaped herself up.

"We're singin' in the rain," they sang, "just singin' in the rain . . ."

I looked at Henry, and he looked at me.

"Come on, boys!" Julia shouted. "It feels so good!"

Henry took off his T-shirt, so I took off mine. Then I took my pants off, and he took off his. Then he took his underwear off, and I took off mine.

If it had been just one of us or two of us, it would have been weird. But with all five of us stark naked, it just felt like the thing to do.

Julia handed me the bar of soap, and the dirt ran off me in little streams. Henry and I joined the girls in the song, shouting, laughing, dancing, and drinking more water as it splashed down on us.

Then, just as suddenly as it arrived, the rain stopped falling. It was like a faucet had been turned off. The storm cloud passed over our heads and the sky was sunny again.

It was weird, too. Before, we had been having fun being silly in the rain. Once it stopped, we were five people standing around with no clothes on. We covered ourselves up the best we could with our hands. Suddenly, I felt cold.

"My uniform is soaked," Arcadia said. "I don't want to put it on again."

"My clothes are filthy," said Julia.

"They're the only clothes we have," Henry said.

"No, they're not," said Mrs. Herschel.

We all looked at her, and one by one we figured out what she meant. Those suitcases we had recovered from the back of the plane were filled with clothes. Dry clothes. Clean clothes.

"What a great idea!" Arcadia said.

"Oh, no," Henry said. "I'm not putting on old lady clothes!"

"Me neither," I agreed.

"Suit yourselves," Mrs. Herschel said. "But as soon as we get back to the campsite, I'm getting dressed."

Julia picked up her clothes. Arcadia and Mrs. Herschel helped her walk. Henry and I didn't have a lot of options. Neither of us memorized the route we took to get there. We didn't want to stand around the forest naked. So we followed them.

By the time we got back to the campsite, we were almost dry. The girls rushed to open up the suitcases and they rifled through the clothes like there was a half-off sale at Target. Mrs. Herschel had no problem finding something that fit her. She put on one of her knitting buddies' outfits and looked pretty much the same as she did before the rain came.

With Julia and Arcadia, it was another story. My eleven-year-old sister—who usually wears blue jeans and T-shirts—looked hilarious dolled up in an old-lady dress. She tried on a few of them before she found one she liked that fit her.

"I feel so grown-up," Julia said, spinning around on her good leg so we could all admire her dress.

Arcadia found a green dress that she liked and slipped it over her head. She looked great, of course. She could wear a trash bag with holes cut out for her arms and she'd still look great.

Henry and I pretty much stood around awkwardly while the girls were playing dress up. Once the three of them had clothes on, it felt even weirder to be standing there naked. In the woods. The two of us. The girls were looking at us. Julia giggled.

"Okay, *okay!*" Henry finally said. "Get me something to wear."

"Way to go, Henry!" Arcadia said.

The three of them dove into the suitcases looking for the perfect outfit for Henry. It seemed like they had even more fun dressing him up than they did dressing themselves.

"Don't you think blue would bring out his eyes?" Arcadia asked, holding a flowered dress up in front of Henry.

"Oh, that is *so* you, Henry!" Julia said.

"Do you think it makes him look fat?" Arcadia asked.

"Let's accessorize him!" said Mrs. Herschel.

"That's enough!" Henry yelled, grabbing the dress. "I'll put it on myself."

Henry put the dress on, and I have to say, it was hilarious. He looked like he escaped from a Monty Python skit.

"Don't slouch," Mrs. Herschel ordered.

"You look ridiculous," I told Henry.

"Not as ridiculous as you, Zimmerman," he replied, adjusting the dress.

He was right. He may have been dolled up like an old lady, but at least he had something on. I was the only one who was standing out there in the middle of the forest, naked.

If I wanted to, I could tell you how the girls went through the suitcases until they found the perfect outfit for me. But frankly, it's just too embarrassing to even discuss. Let's just say I happen to look good in a purple polyester pantsuit.

"You should see yourself, Jimmy," my sister said, trying her best not to laugh. "I wish we had a mirror."

"A mirror?" Arcadia said. "It's too bad we had to break that camera. This should be recorded for posterity."

The two of them had a good laugh over me. Mrs. Herschel didn't laugh, though. She took

Henry and me aside and put an arm around each of our shoulders.

"I must hand it to you gentlemen," she said. "That was not easy to do. But you've earned my respect. It takes a real man to dress up like a girl."

CHAPTER 15:
Food and Shelter

Amazingly, it didn't take long to get used to the fact that Henry and I were walking around in women's clothing. Eighty-year-old women's clothing. Eighty-year-old *dead* women's clothing. Within five minutes, nobody was paying any attention to what I was wearing.

We had more important things to worry about. Julia needed a new splint for her leg, and we all pitched in to make her one. Also, the rain just about knocked our fire out. It was a smoldering mess of soggy ashes. If a plane flew overhead, it wouldn't spot us.

Julia wasn't concerned. She got down on the

ground and poked and prodded until she found an ember that still had some life in it. She added a little tinder and blew on the ember until a few sparks leaped out. The next thing we knew, the fire was blazing again.

When we first crashed, everybody treated my sister like a little kid who needed to be protected. But after seeing the way she started the fire and helped us get water—despite her broken leg—it felt like Julia was the one who was protecting *us*.

"What do you suggest we do now, sweetie?" Mrs. Herschel asked her.

"After that rain," Julia said, "I think we need a shelter."

"You mean we should build a lean-to or something?" asked Arcadia.

"Not exactly," Julia said, limping over to the plane. "Most of the shelter is already here."

She was right, as usual. The rounded shell of

the front of the plane was mostly intact, and it was waterproof. All we had to do was empty it of the first-class seats and we could sleep in there.

The opening was in the back, where the front half of the plane had separated from the rest. There was that gaping hole there, big enough to walk through. It would be a drag to be sleeping in the plane and have a friendly bear or moose or something decide to join us for the night.

It wasn't hard to construct a big leafy door to cover the hole. Me and Henry made a basic four-sided frame from thick branches, using vines to tie it together. Julia, Mrs. Herschel, and Arcadia pulled down a bunch of long, thinner branches from the surrounding trees and criss-crossed them the same way you would weave together a piece of cloth from threads. Mrs. Herschel showed them how to do it, because she had spent her whole lifetime sewing.

Once our door was fairly solid, we stuffed thinner branches with leaves through any holes we could see through. Finally, we lifted the whole panel up and leaned it against the plane to cover the hole. There was a real feeling of accomplishment when we were done.

While the girls were weaving the inside of the door, Henry found a tool kit in the cockpit. He and I used it to remove everything we could from the inside of the plane. It wasn't hard to unscrew the seats. We hauled six of them outside and arranged them in a big circle around the fire. That made enough room on the floor of the plane for all six of us to sleep.

Six of us. I had almost forgotten about David. It had been hours since he stormed out in a huff. David could be a real pain, but he was still my friend and I cared about him. I hoped he was able to drink some water during the downpour.

"Where do you think David is?" I asked Henry.

"He probably killed a bear and he's walking around in a bearskin coat," Henry said. "I'm sure he'll come cruising back here any minute, gloating and telling us about the cool adventure he had."

It took about an hour to strip most of the stuff out of the plane. When we were done, the place looked pretty good. It wasn't a Holiday Inn or anything, but it was home.

"Not a bad shelter," Julia said. "Not bad at all."

"Boy," Henry said, "we sure are lucky this plane happened to crash here. That made building the shelter a lot easier."

"Very funny," I said, flopping into one of the seats around the fire. Henry took the seat next to me, and one by one the girls came over too. I was glad they joined us. I was exhausted, but I didn't want to lie around and rest while the others were working.

"Remember when you said people can survive a month without food?" Arcadia asked Julia.

"Yeah."

"How is that possible?" Arcadia asked. "I mean, my stomach is growling right now, and it's only been a day or so since we crashed."

"Mine too," Henry said. "You think Domino's delivers out here?"

I had almost forgotten about food. I guess my stomach somehow figured out it wasn't going to get anything to eat, so it just closed up shop. But as soon as Arcadia brought it up, the hunger pangs returned. I could really go for Chinese, or Italian.

"If you don't eat," Julia explained, "your digestive system starts to use the nutrients you have in storage. First it devours carbohydrates, then fats. After that, it will get proteins from muscles and tendons."

"Are you suggesting that the body starts *eating* itself?" Henry said.

"I guess you could say that," Julia agreed.

"All those in favor of looking for food, raise your hand," I said.

All five hands went up. Julia added some wood to the fire, we got up, adjusted our dresses, and went shopping for groceries.

Julia said she'd been on the lookout for food when we were searching for water and didn't see any, so we should try the opposite direction. We followed behind her in single file.

"What should we be looking for, sweetie?" Mrs. Herschel asked as we walked through the woods.

"Oh, lots of stuff in nature is edible," Julia replied, pulling up a tall piece of grass and sticking it in her mouth. "Nuts, dandelions, flowers. Just about half of all plant species are edible."

"What about the other half?" I asked.

"They'll kill you," Julia replied.

"That's comforting," Henry said.

"How about acorns?" Mrs. Herschel asked, picking one off the ground. "Can I eat this?"

"Only in an emergency," Julia said. "They have tannic acid, and you'll get a stomach ache if you eat too many."

"Ix-nay on the acorns," Henry said.

Julia stopped beside an evergreen tree and pulled off a pinecone.

"Pine is great," she said, pulling apart the cone and popping something in her mouth. "You can eat the seeds. The needles are a good source of ascorbic acid. And the inner bark is soft and chewy.

"Yeah, I ate a bookcase made from pine once," Henry said. "It was delicious."

"Very funny," Julia said. "You can chew pine resin too, just like gum."

"Only a real sap would do that," Henry said.

"Ugh, I'm not eating something that grew up out of the dirt," Arcadia said.

"Ever eat a potato?" Julia asked.

I was just about hungry enough to eat a tree. But a few yards past the pine tree Arcadia spotted something that looked a lot more appetizing.

"Berries!" she shouted.

Sure enough, there was a bush with purple berries sprouting all over it. We ran over and started to pick them off.

"Wait a minute!" Mrs. Herschel said. "What if these are poisonous?"

We all looked at Julia.

"We should do an edibility test," she said, "but just about all purple, blue, or black berries are edible. The poisonous ones are usually green, yellow, or white."

"How do you know so much?" Henry asked her.

"There are these things called books," Julia replied. "You might want to read one sometime."

"Ooh, *zing*!" Henry said, grabbing his chest like he'd been hit by an arrow.

"What's an edibility test?" Mrs. Herschel asked.

Julia took a couple of the berries off the bush and sniffed them. Then she rubbed them against the inside of her wrist.

"If it's poisonous," she said, "it might cause a reaction."

There was no rash or anything, so Julia rubbed the berries against her lips. They still seemed okay, so she put them in her mouth and held them on her tongue for a few seconds. Then she chewed slowly.

"Seems okay," she said.

Arcadia and Mrs. Herschel and I began to strip berries off the bush and stuff them into our mouths in bunches. They weren't all that sweet, but they were food. Berry juice was running down my chin because I was stuffing my face faster than I could swallow. At some point I noticed that Henry wasn't eating and I asked him why.

"I have my own personal edibility test," he said.

"What's that?" Julia asked.

"If the four of you drop dead," Henry said, "the berries are probably poisonous."

None of us dropped dead, and Henry could only restrain himself for a minute or two longer before he was grabbing for berries and stuffing them into his mouth just like the rest of us.

Julia advised us to take it easy. Our stomachs weren't used to being full. We could always come back for more. Besides, it was starting to get dark out and she didn't want to risk getting lost. We grabbed handfuls and stuffed them in a plastic bag to bring back to the campsite for later.

As we walked back, I actually felt *good* for the first time since the crash. I may have looked ridiculous wearing some old lady's clothes, but I was warm and dry. I'd had something to drink and there was food in my belly. My cuts were healing. My muscles weren't too sore anymore. More than anything else, I was in good company.

Then, about halfway back to camp, I heard a noise in the woods off to the right. It didn't sound like a bird or some animal or the wind whistling between the trees. It was somebody moaning.

As we got closer, I figured out who it was.

David.

CHAPTER 16:
A Darker Dark

All five of us heard the groans in the forest. Nobody needed to say a word. We rushed toward David as a group.

He was sitting on the ground, his back against a tree. His clothes were wet and filthy and his eyes were closed. He was a mess. My skateboard was on the ground next to him.

"David!" I shouted.

"Wake up!" Henry said, shaking him

David turned his head slightly and his eyelids slowly opened, like it was hard work to raise them. He looked at us and smiled a little.

"This is a dream, right, Zimmerman?"

David said. "Or I'm hallucinating."

"No, you're not," I told him.

"Then why are you wearing a dress?" he asked.

"It's not a dress," my sister told him. "It's a pantsuit."

"Whatever," said David.

"It's a long story," Henry said. "What happened to you?"

"I was hungry," David explained, "so hungry. And there was nothing. I ate a bunch of acorns and got sick to my stomach. So I sat down here to rest. I guess I fell asleep. That's when the snake came."

"Snake?" Mrs. Herschel asked. "What snake?"

David pointed to his left and we saw it. About four feet away was a nasty-looking black snake. It had a whitish belly with black markings.

"Eeek!" Arcadia screamed.

"Relax," David said. "It's dead. Lucky I had Zimmerman's board."

Next to my skateboard on the ground was the snake's head. David had chopped it off. There were snake guts stuck to the side of the board. It was gross.

Julia poured some water into David's mouth and Arcadia fed him some berries.

"You'll be okay," Arcadia said. "You're just dehydrated."

"It looks like a rat snake," Julia said, picking the thing up. "It's the largest snake found in Canada."

"How do you know?" Henry asked.

"I read an article in *National Geographic Kids*," she replied.

"There's one more thing," David told us. "Before I could nail him with the board, he sort of . . . bit me."

"What!?"

"On the leg," David said. "He got me pretty good."

We rolled up David's pants leg and found puncture marks above his left ankle.

"When did it happen?" Julia asked urgently.

"Not long ago," David said. "Fifteen minutes I think, maybe half an hour. I lost track of time."

I didn't know a whole lot about snakes, but I remembered hearing about some species whose venom is so powerful it could kill a man in minutes. David could die. Maybe he knew it. For the first time, I noticed his eyes were watery.

"I'm sorry," David said, trying not to cry.

"What for?" I asked.

"I shouldn't have left you guys," he said. "I was a jerk. This was my own fault."

"Forget it," Arcadia said. "You're going to be okay."

"I saw a James Bond movie once," Henry said. "This girl got bitten by a snake or a sea urchin or something and James Bond sucked the venom out of her foot."

I didn't really want to suck on David's foot, but I would if it would save his life.

"Sucking out venom isn't a good idea," Julia told us. "If you get it in your mouth, it can enter your bloodstream."

"So what do we do?" I asked. "He could die any minute!"

"Calm down," Julia told me. "There are thousands of species of snakes, and almost all of them are harmless. Hardly anybody ever dies from snakebite."

There was some swelling around the bite mark, but David didn't feel weakness or numbness in his leg. Julia concluded that the bite wasn't poisonous. But to be on the safe side, she said we should immobilize David's leg and keep

167

it lower than his heart. She squeezed the skin around the wound to push any venom out. Arcadia got some vines and tied them around David's leg a couple of inches above and below the bite to slow the spread of any poison. Then she cleaned the puncture marks with water and wrapped a few big leaves around as a home-made bandage.

The water and berries were already making David feel better. Henry and I helped him to his feet. Julia grabbed the longer piece of the snake.

"Souvenir?" I asked her.

"No," she replied. "Dinner."

David was able to walk back to the campsite. He seemed a lot quieter than he ever did before. I think what had happened threw a scare into him. He realized how lucky he was that we found him.

"Nice," he said when we reached camp and saw the airplane seats arranged in a circle around the fire. "I like what you've done to the place."

He didn't even put up a fight when Mrs. Herschel took off his clothes and gave him a dress to put on. We parked David in one of the seats around the fire to rest. Julia found a rock with a sharp edge, and she used it to skin and gut the snake.

"Are you really going to eat that thing?" Arcadia asked. "It's gross!"

"I'll take your share if you don't want it," Julia said.

I didn't exactly want to eat snake, but I wanted to eat *something*. Beggars can't be choosers, as they say. I found a long stick and gave it to Julia. She stuck the sharp end into the fire briefly to harden it, then she cut a piece of snake off and put it on the end of the stick. She held it over the fire, turning it like she was toasting a marshmallow.

"Who wants the first piece?" she asked, blowing on it to cool it off.

Nobody volunteered, so Julia shrugged and popped the snake into her mouth. We all looked at her, half expecting her to throw up, or keel over, or something.

"Tastes like chicken," she said, putting another piece on the end of the stick.

That was good enough for me. I got the next piece, and it not only tasted like chicken, it tasted like the best chicken I had ever eaten. Julia roasted pieces for Henry, David, and Mrs. Herschel. When he got his piece, David said, "He bit me, so I'm biting him back."

In the end, even Arcadia decided to have a piece of the snake, grimacing the whole time she chewed it. After that, it was gone. You don't get a whole lot of meat out of a snake.

It was completely dark now. There was no visible moon in the sky. The only light was our crackling fire.

When were we going to get *rescued*? I

wondered as I poked at the fire with a stick. People were out there in the woods looking for us, I tried to convince myself. It was only a matter of time.

The sky was a different dark, a darker dark from any dark I had ever seen. And I knew why. We were so far from any city. Bright lights make it hard to see the night sky. So does pollution from cars and factories. There were no cars or factories or cities where we were. It was perfectly dark.

"This is the life," Henry said, leaning his seat back. "I'm not even sure I want to be rescued."

"I do," I said. "I miss skateboarding."

I don't think I had *ever* gone so long without skating. I wondered how long you have to stop before you forget all your tricks. It occurred to me that if we never got rescued, I would never skate again. That would be horrible.

There was an opening in the trees over our heads, and we could see the stars. Each of us leaned back our seats to look. It was calming, peaceful.

"Do you think there's anybody out there?" Julia asked. "I mean, life?"

"Maybe somebody's out there looking at Earth right now," Henry said, "and wondering if there's life *here*."

"Could be," said Mrs. Herschel.

"Where do you think it ends?" I asked. "Outer space, I mean."

"It goes on forever," David said.

"It's got to end somewhere," Henry said.

"Why?" David replied. "Maybe it's infinite."

I was afraid David and Henry were going to get into another religious argument. But the sky was just so beautiful, I don't think either of them wanted to debate how it started or where it was going.

"Do you think they're looking for us?" Julia asked.

"Sure they are," said Arcadia.

"They should have found us by now," Henry said.

"They're coming," Mrs. Herschel said. "We just need to be patient. Can you see the North Star? It's also called Polaris."

The sky was just a big mass of twinkling stars to me. I couldn't identify anything. Mrs. Herschel helped us find the Big Dipper, and told us to line up the two stars at the far edge of the dipper and extend the line to the North Star.

"The Big Dipper rotates around Polaris like an hour hand on a clock," she explained.

"I see it," Julia said.

So did I. Mrs. Herschel showed us where Venus was, and told us the Milky Way is made up of a hundred billion stars.

"When we look at a star that's a million light

years from Earth," she told us, "we're actually looking at light that left that star a million years ago."

"Wow," we all said.

"So does that mean light leaving a star today might not reach Earth for a million years?" asked Henry.

"That's right," Mrs. Herschel said.

"Wow."

"How do you know so much about astronomy?" David asked.

"It runs in my family," Mrs. Herschel said. "My great-great-great-grandfather was an astronomer."

"Really?" Arcadia said.

"Indeed," Mrs. Herschel replied. "William Herschel. He was quite famous in his day."

None of us had ever heard of William Herschel, and Mrs. Herschel seemed a little disappointed.

"In fact, he discovered one of the planets," she said.

"You're kidding me!" said David.

"Not at all," Mrs. Herschel insisted.

"Which one?" Henry asked. "Venus? Jupiter?"

"Uranus."

Well, it took about five minutes for the rest of us to stop giggling. Mrs. Herschel rolled her eyes, like she'd been through this many times before.

But what did she expect? Uranus! It's the funniest planet, easy. It may be the funniest word in the English language. All you have to do is say it and people crack up.

"It's not that bloody funny," Mrs. Herschel said while we were doubled over.

"I can't believe it," Henry said. "Your great-great-great-grandfather discovered Uranus." He had fallen off his seat and was rolling around on the ground, holding his sides.

Scientists have proven that it's impossible to say the word "Uranus" in any group of people without at least a few of them snickering. *Any* word that sounds like "anus" is funny. A couple of years ago Burger King had a sandwich they called the "Angus," and everyone at my school insisted on calling it the "anus burger." That's probably why Burger King pulled it off the market.

"I always thought that naming the planet Uranus was the greatest practical joke in history," Henry said, "and here I am, sitting next to a lady who's related to the guy who actually did it."

"Oh, no," Mrs. Herschel said. "William Herschel discovered Uranus, but he didn't name it. He wanted to name it in honor of King George. But some German bloke dubbed it Uranus, and it somehow stuck."

"What does Uranus really mean, anyway?"

Arcadia asked, trying to be serious.

"The ancient Greeks had a god of the sky," Mrs. Herschel said. "It was called Ouranos."

Ouranos?

Well, the five of us didn't stop laughing for another five minutes.

CHAPTER 17:
Macho, Macho Men

We finished stargazing, and Julia said she would "bank the fire" before we went to sleep. None of us knew what she was talking about, so she showed us. She covered the fire pit lightly with ashes. The flames were snuffed out, but Julia said that in the morning it would be easy to take off the ashes, lay on a little tinder, and blow on the smoldering embers to get the fire back to life again. When did my sister get to be so smart?

When we woke up that next morning, Julia's leg felt a little better and David had recovered from his encounter with the snake. I guess it wasn't poisonous after all.

The snake. Just thinking about it got my stomach rumbling again. The berries we had found were good, but they didn't satisfy my appetite. I felt a general weakness that I wasn't used to. My body was crying out for some milk, or cheese, or meat. I'd eat another snake in a minute if we could catch one.

"We need protein," I said to nobody in particular. "A person can't live on berries."

"Well, there's no protein out here," Henry said. "So just forget about it."

"That's not altogether true," Julia told him. "Did you ever try entomophagous cuisine?"

"Is that like Ethiopian?" Arcadia asked. "I went to an Ethiopian restaurant in New York once. You eat with your hands."

"Not exactly," Julia said. She went over to a fallen tree at the edge of the campsite. The bark was loose and rotting away. Julia peeled back a piece of the wood. "See? This place is *crawling* with protein."

There were all kinds of creepy-crawly things in there.

"Ugh! Don't even think about it!" Arcadia said. "I'm not eating bugs!"

"Why not?" Julia asked. "You ate snake."

"Snake is meat," David said.

"Yeah," Henry said. "Bugs are . . . bugs!"

"Don't be silly," Julia said. "You eat lobsters. They're weird looking. You eat shrimp. You eat cows and chickens and pigs. What's the difference?"

"I can't eat bugs," Henry said. "It's against my religion."

"You're an atheist, you foon," David said.

"Well, I'm on a bug-free diet," Henry said. "Doctor's orders."

"Bugs have more protein per pound than fish or meat," Julia told us. "They have a lot of vitamins, too."

"You probably take one-a-day cockroaches," Henry cracked.

"When did *you* ever eat a bug?" I asked my sister.

"In Girl Scouts," she said. "I earned a badge for entomophagy. We tried cicadas, locusts, grubs, slugs, ants, maggots . . ."

"Eeeewww," we all went.

"Remind me not to join the Girl Scouts," Henry said.

"The grasshoppers were the best," Julia continued. "We roasted them. You have to cut away their wings and legs first. They're crunchy. Earthworms are good too. You just remove the shell and head, and then you mash them up in a stew."

"Thanks for sharing that with us," Arcadia said. "If you don't mind, I need to go vomit now."

"Squirt is goofing on us," David said. "She never ate a bug."

"Oh, no?"

Julia reached down and picked up some little disgusting crawling critter with her fingertips. Its little legs were flailing around. Then she popped the thing in her mouth like it was candy.

"Eeeewww!"

"You're sick!"

"You have mental problems!"

"There goes my appetite."

"I can't believe we come from the same parents," I told my sister.

"Delicious!" Julia said, smacking her lips. "Tastes like a Tic Tac."

"Really?" Arcadia asked.

"Sure," said Julia. "Try one."

Julia found another little critter and held it out for Arcadia.

"I don't want to touch it," Arcadia said.

"Open your mouth and close your eyes," Julia told her. When Arcadia did as she was told, Julia put the critter on her tongue. Arcadia closed her mouth. We could see her chewing.

"Ugh!" she said, spitting the thing out. "I think I'm going to die!"

Julia tried to get the rest of us to try a bug, but there were no takers.

I really wanted to. I knew in my mind that there was no difference between eating a chicken and eating an insect. But I just couldn't bring myself to do it. The thought of it made me nauseous. Maybe if I had grown up eating insects instead of chicken it would have been a different story. But I think we all admired Julia for what she did. It took guts to eat, uh, bug guts.

"We don't have to eat bugs," David said. "I have another idea."

At that point, I was open to anything.

"Let's hear it," Mrs. Herschel said.

"I've seen a lot of squirrels running around,"

David said. "These woods must be swarming with small game."

It was true. None of them had ever run into the Deathtrap that David made after the crash, but there were squirrels scampering all over the place.

"I'm not eating squirrel!" Arcadia said.

"You said you wouldn't eat snake," I reminded her.

"How are we going to catch a bloody squirrel anyway?" Mrs. Herschel asked.

"Let's go hunting!" David said.

"Yeah!" said Henry. "We'll hunt for meat!"

Let's just say I had mixed feelings about the whole hunting-for-meat idea. I was hungry, that was for sure. It didn't look like we were going to be rescued anytime soon, and I had to eat something besides berries. I had eaten plenty of animals in my life, but I didn't particularly want to kill any personally.

On the other hand, David and Henry were all gung ho to go hunting. At least David wasn't being obnoxious about it, bossing everyone around the way he did before the snake incident.

"Yeah," I said, pretending to be enthusiastic, "let's go hunt for meat."

Julia laughed. "I remember the last time you hunted for meat. It was at the supermarket. Mom told you to get a half a pound of roast beef."

The girls had a good laugh, but David and Henry were serious. Henry had taken a class in survival once, and he knew how to make some weapons. The three of us went out into the woods to search for the right sticks.

Under Henry's direction, we made two spears. I have a pretty good arm, so they let me carry the spears. David found a piece of wood that was flattened and curved a little bit like a boomerang. Henry said it could be thrown sidearm and it would fly like an airplane wing. So that became David's weapon.

Henry found a strong, flexible branch and made it into a primitive bow using dental floss as the string. We each made an arrow for the bow, and Henry even found some bird feathers and stuck them into cracks at the end of the arrows to help them fly straight. It was kind of fun. I was starting to get into the whole idea of going on a hunt with the guys. As long as we didn't actually kill anything.

"I wish I had a hatchet," I said, while we were working on our weapons.

"We have something better," David said. "Our brains. Our ingenuity. Our intelligence."

"I still wish I had a hatchet."

"We have opposable thumbs too," Henry said, giving me two thumbs up. "That's what separates us from the animals."

Our weapons completed, we went back to the campsite to harden the spears and arrow points in the fire.

"Nice spears, Brittney," my sister told me.

"Now, don't you big strong men worry about us womenfolk," Mrs. Herschel told us, putting on a really bad, fake Western accent. "We'll stay right here and tend to the young 'uns."

Arcadia and Julia thought that was hilarious.

"Didn't you guys forget to put on your loincloths?" Arcadia asked.

"Yes," said Mrs. Herschel, "maybe you want to do a little macho war dance to prepare for the big hunt."

"They'll probably get lost in the woods and I'll have to rescue them," said my sister.

"Go ahead and laugh," Henry said. "Just be ready for a big feast when we get back."

"Bring back a quarter of a pound of ham,

Jimmy," Julia called as we left, "and a quart of milk."

"You're our heroes!" called Arcadia as we marched off into the woods.

Their jokes didn't bother us. Even if we didn't bring back any animals, it was fun traipsing around hunting for them. We were careful to keep track of our direction. Coming back empty-handed wouldn't be humiliating, but getting lost and having Julia rescue us would be.

"Maybe we'll bag a deer!" I said soon after we set out.

"Don't be ridiculous," Henry replied. "Where would we get a bag big enough to hold a deer?"

"Quiet, you foons!" David said. "You'll scare the animals away."

I held the spears up at shoulder height so I would be ready if anything less than human ran by. We tried to walk gently so the leaves and sticks underfoot wouldn't make too much noise.

In the survival class, Henry told us he learned that you're supposed to keep downwind from an animal you're stalking. That way, it can't pick up your scent. How are you supposed to do that, I wondered? I guess you're supposed to circle around them or something. It didn't make a lot of sense to me.

Henry also told us to keep perfectly still if we saw an animal. Some species, like deer, only see movement. If you stand still, you're virtually invisible to them.

We walked around for quite a while, and we didn't see another living creature. The squirrels must have been hiding. I was getting tired and began to question the whole idea of the hunt. We needed to get some calories in us, but we were burning a lot of calories trying to find some. If we didn't come back with anything to eat, we would have been better off if we had just stayed at the campsite.

And then, about an hour into the hunt, David stopped dead in his tracks and held up a hand to signal us to stop.

"What is it?" Henry whispered.

"Shhh," David said. "Don't move. Eyes right."

I looked to my right and saw it. A deer. It was a big one, about thirty yards away. Its head was in a bush. This was one beautiful animal. Suddenly I could hear my own heart pounding.

"Wow," Henry whispered. "He's ours for the taking."

"Nobody shoot until I say so," David whispered. "We'll triple our chances if we all fire at the same time."

"What if it attacks us?" I asked.

"They only attack if they think their babies are threatened," Henry whispered.

The deer ate some leaves off the bush, and

then picked its head up. It looked like it was staring right at us, but it didn't run away. It must not have noticed us. The muscles in my arms and legs were getting sore from holding still for so long.

"If he puts his head back in the bush," David whispered, "I'll count to three and then we'll fire, okay?"

"Okay," Henry replied.

"I don't know if I can do it," I said.

"What's the matter?" David asked. "You think we're too far away?"

"No," I said. "What if that deer is somebody's mother?"

"We don't have time for that carp now, Zimmerman," David told me. "All living creatures have a sacred right to fulfill the measure of their creation."

"Oh no, here comes a religious lecture," Henry said.

"It's not religious," David whispered. "We're hunting for survival. We don't want trophies, we want dinner. It's a mature relationship with nature. Humans are further up the food chain than deer. It's our right to kill them. We have intelligence. We have opposable thumbs."

"So because they don't have thumbs we should be allowed to kill them?" I asked.

"Be wimps if you want to," David said. "I'm getting dinner."

"He put his face back in the bush!" Henry said, almost too loudly.

"Hey, I think I see his thumb!"

"Ready?" David said. "One. Two. Three. Fire!"

I brought back my spear to throw it, but at the same time Henry's bow and arrow misfired. The dental floss string must have come out of the groove in the arrow, because the arrow flew backward and hit me in the shoulder. I fell over and bumped against David as he was trying to throw his boomerang thing.

"Ow, my shoulder!" I cried.

"You foon!" David yelled. "You almost took my eye out!"

"It wasn't my fault!" Henry said.

The deer scampered off into the woods. David cursed. He wanted to track the deer and chase it, but Henry and I were too tired. My shoulder was bleeding, too, from the arrow.

Exhausted, we began the long hike back to the campsite.

"What are we going to tell the girls?" I asked as we stopped to pick some berries along the way. "They'll never let us hear the end of this."

"We'll tell 'em we got attacked by a bear," Henry suggested. "We fought it off, but he scraped you on the shoulder with his claw and he got away. We were brave warriors."

We rehearsed the story on our way back to the campsite. But as it turned out, we didn't have to tell the girls anything. Because as we approached the campsite, Arcadia was signaling us frantically.

"Shhh!" she said. "We've got an animal!"

CHAPTER 18:
Tastes Like Chicken

We tiptoed the rest of the way to the campsite, where my sister and Mrs. Herschel were crouching behind the plane. They looked like they were playing hide-and-go-seek. I peered over to where they seemed to be staring, and a few yards from the campsite, next to a tree, there was a big, fat, rabbit.

"How did you catch it?" Henry whispered to Arcadia.

"We didn't catch it yet," she replied. "We're *trying* to catch it."

There was some kind of a weird apparatus next to the tree. The girls had turned my skateboard wheels up and stuck a stick under one end of it. Tied to the bottom of the stick was a piece of dental floss, and I could see it extended on the ground to where Julia and Mrs. Herschel were hiding. Lodged between the front and back wheels of the skateboard was a big rock, I guess to give it weight.

"That's called a deadfall," Henry whispered. "You yank the stick out with the string, and the weight falls on the animal."

"You mean we just spent an hour wandering around the woods for nothing and we could have caught a rabbit right here?" I asked.

"I didn't think of it," Henry admitted.

"Yer a foon," David said.

The rabbit was about two feet away from the deadfall, and it was sniffing around the ground. I couldn't tell what was under the skateboard, but it was a little white glop.

"What's she using for bait?" David asked Arcadia.

"Toothpaste," she replied.

"Do rabbits like toothpaste?" I asked.

"We're going to find out," Arcadia replied.

The rabbit couldn't seem to make up its mind about going under the skateboard. Maybe the toothpaste wasn't interesting enough. Too bad we didn't have better bait, I thought. But then, if we had better bait, we probably would have eaten it ourselves.

"Come on, Mr. Rabbit," Henry whispered. "You should brush your teeth twice a day."

Julia was being patient. If she pulled the string too soon, the rabbit would run away. She had a good view of it from behind the plane, and Mrs. Herschel was right next to her, whispering in her ear.

Finally the rabbit nosed forward a few steps to get a sniff of the toothpaste.

"Now!" Mrs. Herschel said, and Julia yanked the dental floss. The stick popped out and the skateboard came crashing down on top of the rabbit. The rock held it down.

"Got him!" Julia shouted, and we all started cheering.

"Ooh, another extreme-sports accident!" Henry shouted, like he was an X Games announcer. "That just shows how dangerous skateboards can be."

"Especially if you're a rabbit," I said.

"Or a snake," added David.

"This wouldn't have happened if the rabbit had been wearing a helmet," Henry noted.

It occurred to me that there were probably more animal guts on my skateboard than any other skateboard in the world.

I felt sorry for the little guy if, in fact, it was a guy. But after all, it was his own fault. Nobody forced him to go under the skateboard. He did it of his own free will.

"Who wants to put him out of his misery?" asked Julia.

"It's not my cup of tea," Mrs. Herschel said. "You may have the honors, sweetie."

"I'd love to help, but I have to do my homework," said Henry.

"I'll help," David said, and I breathed a big sigh of relief. I can't even look when the doctor gives me a shot. No way was I going to kill a rabbit.

"We'll need one of those sharp pieces of metal from the plane," David told Julia.

Henry, Arcadia, Mrs. Herschel and I—the big chickens—hustled over to the far end of the campsite so we wouldn't have to hear the tortured screams of protest from the poor innocent creature who was about to have his guts ripped out by my friend and my sadistic, demented sister.

"Oh, the poor bunny!" Arcadia said.

"We should hold a memorial service for it," I suggested.

"Yeah," Henry said, "right after we eat."

"I don't think I can eat a bunny," Arcadia fretted.

"Don't think of it as a bunny," I told her. "It's a rabbit."

"It's a *bunny* rabbit!" Arcadia said, nearly in tears.

"Maybe it would help if you thought of it as an *evil* bunny rabbit," Henry suggested.

"Oh, don't be silly, dear," Mrs. Herschel said. "You ate snake. You ate a bug."

"I spit the bug out," Arcadia corrected her.

It took a while for Julia and David to kill, skin, and do all those other nasty things to the rabbit before we could eat it. Henry suggested we pass the time by playing the license plate game, and since Mrs. Herschel didn't get the joke, we had to explain to her what the license plate game was and why it would be funny to play it out in the woods. Mrs. Herschel said we were "daft Yanks" and

took it upon herself to explain the rules of cricket to us, which made absolutely no sense at all. But it did help pass the time.

"Dinnertime!" Julia finally announced. "You wimps can come back now."

"Great," I said. "I'm so hungry I could eat a rabbit."

The sheet of metal was laying by the fire with a bunch of thin strips of meat lined up perfectly in rows. It was impressive.

"*That* was the rabbit?" Mrs. Herschel asked. "How did you do that?"

"It was simple, really," Julia said. "First we sliced the loose fur from his back and peeled the rest of his skin off carefully . . ."

". . . and then we cut off his feet and severed his head," explained David. "We hung him upside down to drain the blood, cut his throat, removed his guts, and sliced him into cutlets."

"Great," I said. "I'm not hungry anymore."

But of course I was. While Julia and David wiped the rabbit guts off their hands with leaves, Henry added enough wood to the fire to get a good blaze going. Arcadia and Mrs. Herschel gathered some long sticks. We attached the rabbit cutlets and began to roast them.

We didn't have any spices or seasonings, but the smell of cooking meat was wonderful anyway. Julia said we should be careful not to overcook it, because the more you heat something the more nutrition is lost. But we were all a little afraid of germs and bacteria, so we burned the meat a little.

I couldn't wait anymore. The smell was overpowering. I took my stick out of the fire and blew on the meat to cool it down. Then I took a bite.

I've been to a few nice restaurants in my time. You know, those places where you have to

wear your good clothes and your parents make you put the cloth napkins in your lap? Well, the food in those places was nothing compared with the taste of fresh rabbit roasted out in the woods. I had never tasted anything so delicious in my life.

"It tastes like chicken," said Henry.

"It tastes better than chicken," I said.

For the most part, we didn't say anything. We were enjoying the food too much. The only thing that would have made it better would be a big glop of mashed potatoes on the side. Or french fries. And a drink. A soda. That would have been perfect.

When we finished all the cutlets, the six of us just sat back on our seats and relaxed.

"I couldn't eat another bite," Arcadia said.

"Do you know how much food the average person eats in one year?" Julia asked. "A ton."

Unbelievable. We had eaten almost nothing

in the last few days. Back home, I took food for granted. Any time I felt a rumble in my stomach, I could just go to the kitchen and grab something from the fridge. I never once thought about where the food came from, whether it was grown from the ground or killed or how it was prepared. Maybe the rabbit tasted so good because we caught it, prepared it, and cooked it ourselves. Or some of us did, anyway.

Arcadia and my sister got up and went inside the plane. They came out a minute later with a platter and what looked like a chocolate cake on it.

"Happy birthday to you," they began to sing. "Happy birthday to you. Happy birthday, Mrs. Her . . . schel. Happy birthday to you."

Mrs. Herschel was beaming from ear to ear.

"Is that a real cake?" I asked, incredulous.

"Of course not," Arcadia said. "We made it out of mud."

"How did you know it was my birthday?" asked Mrs. Herschel.

"You told us you were going to turn eighty in a few days," Arcadia said. "That was a few days ago. So we figured you must be eighty."

"We wish we had candles for you to blow out," Julia said.

"Forget the candles," Henry said. "I wish you had a real cake."

"Well, I think it's lovely," Mrs. Herschel said. "Thank you. I'll always remember where I was the day I turned eighty."

CHAPTER 19:
An Opportunity

It had been three or four days. We didn't know exactly, because we didn't know how long we had been unconscious after the crash.

We started keeping track of the days, carving a line to represent each day on a tree trunk near the campsite. It was Mrs. Herschel's idea. That's what prisoners in jails do, she told us. Otherwise they go crazy. After a while you forget what day of the week it is, and how long you've been locked up. Eventually you lose your mind.

We were beginning to settle into a routine, the six of us. Every morning, the first person awake would get the fire stoked up and throw some wet leaves on it to produce smoke in case a plane flew overhead. One by one we would go to the "bathroom." Arcadia liked to pick berries for breakfast. Mrs. Herschel would lead us all in yoga and stretching exercises. Sleeping on the floor of the plane left us all achy in the morning.

Julia built a new deadfall so that maybe we could trap another rabbit or small animal. Once we had the taste of meat, we all wanted more.

We had seen no sign of rescue since that plane flew overhead a few days earlier. I, for one, was beginning to give up hope that anybody would find us out in the middle of nowhere. I didn't tell the others, but I couldn't stop thinking that maybe the world had stopped looking for us. Maybe everybody assumed we were dead. People don't usually survive plane crashes. I know that after a certain amount of time, rescue teams give up because the chances of finding survivors becomes smaller and smaller. They can't keep searching indefinitely. Rescue missions cost a lot of money.

I was getting depressed. I think we all were.

David suggested that maybe we should leave the campsite and start hiking south. We could use the sun to navigate, he said. If we could cover twenty or thirty miles a day, in ten days we would be 200-300 miles south. Eventually we'd have to stumble upon a town or some evidence of civilization.

We talked it over as a group. The rest of us were inclined to stay at our campsite, where we had shelter, fire, food, and water. Henry said one of the first rules of survival is to stay where you are. If you go wandering all over the place, it's even harder for rescue teams to find you. And who knows what you might encounter in your travels?

We voted 5-1 to stay put. I thought David

might go strike out on his own the way he did earlier, but he didn't. After his experience with the snake, I guess he decided it would be safer to stick with the group.

After the morning chores were finished, there wasn't a whole lot to do. Henry was sitting in one of the airplane seats and staring into the fire. He looked like he was lost in thought. I plopped down in the seat next to him.

I didn't know what Henry was thinking about, but I was thinking about home and what was going on back there. If I was home, I could just skateboard into town and get an ice-cream cone. That would taste so good. What were my parents doing right now, I wondered? They were probably at work. If only I had a webcam or something and could see them on the screen. Did they miss me and Julia? Did they hold a memorial service for us? Did they already have a yard sale and sell all my things? They'd better not sell my skateboard stuff—the magazines, the posters, my old boards, wheels, and bearings.

"Man, I miss skating," I said, and Henry nodded.

"Y'know, skaters look at the world differently," Henry said, poking a stick absentmindedly into the fire. "To most people, a skateboard is just a piece of wood with wheels on it. It's a toy. To me, it's like an extension of my body."

I knew exactly what he meant. When regular people look at a set of stairs, all they see is a way to get from one floor to the next one. But when you're a skater, you look at a set of stairs and you see an opportunity. You wonder if it's possible to jump those stairs. Is it possible to grind that banister? Every ledge, every curb, every rail is a potential skate spot. A challenge.

David parked himself in the seat next to Henry.

"Hey," he said, "remember the time we tried to skate off the garage onto the roof of the old Cadillac that Henry's dad was fixing up?"

Just thinking about it made me smile. We had been shooting our *Woodpushers Gone Wild* skate video. We were sure it would be so impressive that one of the skateboard companies would *have* to sponsor us. We got a big black umbrella that we were using like a parachute. David skateboarded off the garage holding the umbrella and tried to land on the car.

"You almost died, if I recall," Henry said.

"Yeah," David said, laughing. "It was great."

"I'd give anything to skate right now," I said.

"I'd cut off one of my fingers to skate right now," Henry said.

"I'd cut off my ear," David said. "That's what Vincent van Gogh did."

"He was insane," I told them.

The sun had positioned itself right between two branches and it was shining in my eyes. I closed them so I wouldn't be blinded. When I turned my head a little and opened them again, there was a bright yellow afterimage of the sun superimposed over our plane. It almost looked like the rays of the sun were shooting out of the plane itself. It was a startling image, and it seemed almost spiritual, or mystical, or something. It was like a higher power was trying to send me a message.

I thought about it for a moment or two, and then I realized something that I had never noticed before.

The shape of an airplane's body is identical to the shape of a halfpipe.

CHAPTER 20:
The Halfpipe

It was like a vision, a bolt out of the blue! It was like that cornball moment in every movie when the hero suddenly has some brilliant idea or insight and you hear a choir of angels singing.

I looked at the plane again. If the top was cut off, it would be the shape of the letter *U*. I was sitting not more than ten yards from a perfect halfpipe! It had been right under our noses this whole time! How did I not see it before?

"Hey!" I said to the guys. "Does that look familiar to you?"

"Does *what* look familiar to us?" David asked.

"The plane!" I said excitedly. "The shape of the plane!"

"Yeah," Henry said, "it's shaped just like an airplane. Remarkable!"

"It's shaped like something else too," I told them. "Don't you see it? It's a halfpipe!"

"Zimmerman, you're delirious because you never went this long without skating," David said. "You're starting to hallucinate."

"No, he's *right!*" Henry said, getting up to look at the plane more closely. "If we stripped off the outside shell, it would make a perfect halfpipe!"

Finally, even David saw what we were talking about. We all went to the plane and ran our hands over the surface.

"We could skate this thing!" the three of us said at the same time.

It would be simple. All we'd need to do would be to remove the outside layer of metal, turn it upside down, lay it on the ground, and prop both sides up to hold it in place. It shouldn't take too long. We had already found the toolbox in the cockpit and used it to remove the seats.

There was just one problem. We were using the plane as a place to sleep. It was our shelter. The girls probably wouldn't take too kindly to the idea of ripping it apart so we could build a halfpipe.

"No way they'll go for it," I said.

"Hey, there are three of us and three of them," David whispered so the girls couldn't hear. "All we have to do is convince one of them and we'll have a majority."

"Listen to Mr. Democracy," Henry said. "Aren't you the one who didn't approve of voting?"

"Well, I changed my mind," David said.

So we went over to the girls. Henry and David agreed that I should do the talking because, they said, I have "a way with words."

"We were thinking," I began, "that we only use the plane as a place to sleep. That's a big waste. So, uh, you wouldn't mind if we sort of . . . took it apart and made it into a half-pipe, would you? All in favor, raise your hand."

Me, David, and Henry raised our hands.

"What?!" my sister exclaimed. "Are you crazy?"

Right away, Julia and Arcadia started in whining and being all negative about my great idea.

"We have more important things to do. . . . What would shield us from the rain? . . . Where would we sleep? . . . How would you take off the metal? . . . You'll fall down and get hurt. . . . We have no medical training. . . ." And so on. Those two are no fun at all.

"May I ask one question?" said Mrs. Herschel.

"Shoot," Henry said.

"What's a halfpipe?"

We explained to Mrs. Herschel what a half-pipe was. At first she looked at us just like we must have looked to her when she was trying to explain cricket. But eventually, she seemed to grasp the idea that you skate up and down and up and down the halfpipe for no other reason than the thrill of it. After listening to our explanation, astonishingly, she raised her hand.

"I think it's a smashing idea!" Mrs. Herschel said. "You boys have worked hard. You deserve to have a little fun."

"All right!" we yelled, high-fiving each other. "Majority rules!"

Julia and Arcadia weren't happy, but what could they do? We had voted on it.

David, Henry, and I hauled out the toolbox and got to work building the halfpipe right away. It wasn't as hard as we thought it would be. There was a gadget in the toolbox that made it easy to loosen and tighten the rivets that held the metal skin on the body of the plane. We only had one, so David was assigned the job of peeling the metal plates off. While he did that, Henry and I built a simple ladder out of tree branches and vines so we would be able to climb up to the top of the half-pipe.

As it turned out, removing the metal from the plane wasn't going to ruin our shelter after all. There was another layer underneath that would protect us from the rain. So Julia and Arcadia weren't so upset about our little project. In fact, they started to help. Julia kept us going with berries and some nuts she found while we worked. Arcadia came up with the idea of making a helmet and kneepads for us out of the bark of a tree. She said she could use vines to strap them on.

"I'm not wearing some lame helmet made out

of tree bark," David complained when Arcadia suggested the idea.

"Hey, bark helmets are cool," Henry said. "I bet in a couple of years everybody will be wearing bark helmets."

David didn't peel *all* the metal off the plane. He just took off enough to make a ten-foot half-pipe that was about six feet wide. We put the pieces together on the ground next to the plane and tightened the rivets as much as we could with our fingers. Then David used the tool to make each rivet good and tight.

Finally, as the sun was beginning to sink in the afternoon sky, our halfpipe was done. We were exhausted, but it was beautiful. We checked all the rivets to make sure none of them were loose. We slid the whole thing over until it was braced by the plane. We probably should have called it a day and tested out the halfpipe in the morning, but none of us wanted to wait.

We had worked so hard building it. We wanted to skate.

I got out my trusty titanium skateboard. This board had already come in handy so many times, it occurred to me. I used it to bash that hijacker over the head so we could take control of the plane. The board saved my life when the plane crashed and I went flying through the windshield. We used it to help start the fire. David killed the snake with it. The girls used it to trap the rabbit. And now we were finally going to use it for the purpose it was intended. To *skate*.

The question was, who would go first? It was my board, of course. Obviously, I should get the first turn.

"Firsts!" David called. "I got dibs."

"Why should *you* get to go first?" Henry said. "It's Zimmerman's board."

"If it wasn't for me, we never would have fought back when they hijacked the plane,"

David said. "We'd all be dead right now."

"Oh, yeah?" Henry said, "If it wasn't for me we'd be dead right now too. I'm the one who landed the plane. Maybe I should go first."

"I'm the one who thought of building a half-pipe," I chimed in.

"And it's my brother's board," added Julia.

We had a pretty good argument going when Henry suddenly stopped talking. I looked at him. His face was pale and his mouth was open. He was looking over my shoulder. I turned around to see what he was looking at.

Arcadia let out a scream. There was a guy standing there!

CHAPTER 21:
Heroes

"Who are *you*?"

He was a big guy, even taller than my dad. He was wearing a uniform and one of those hats that Dudley Do-Right wore in those old cartoons.

"James Cavanaugh, Royal Canadian Mounted Police," the guy said, sticking out his hand.

"What are you doing out here?" I asked.

"Well, I believe I'm rescuing you," he said. "Sorry we weren't here sooner. It's quite remote. The roads were blocked . . . had a heckuva time getting here."

At first we couldn't comprehend this stranger in our midst. It had been so long since we'd seen another human being, we didn't quite know what to make of him. But that only lasted a few seconds.

"We're saved!" everybody started screaming. "Yipee! We're going home!"

The six of us were all jumping up and down and hugging each other as if we had won the Super Bowl or something.

"We just about gave up hope of finding you folks alive," the officer told us once we had calmed down. "We've been looking high and low for you."

"Maybe you should have looked in the middle," said Henry.

"Say, if you don't mind my asking," the officer said, "why are you fellows dressed in women's clothes?"

"It's a long story," we all said.

We were thrilled to be rescued, of course. Soon we'd be back home with our parents, our pets, our stuff. I could sleep in my own bed without worrying about a bear attacking me. I could eat a pizza. I could eat a *real* chocolate cake. Life would return to normal. Even going back to school in September would be great.

But something was bothering me. Something wasn't right. I guess we all felt it.

"Uh, officer," Henry asked, "would you mind giving us a little more time here?"

"You don't want to be rescued yet?"

"First we need to skate our halfpipe," David told him.

"Yeah!" Henry and I agreed.

The officer said he understood, and told us to take all the time we needed.

"Okay," I said. "Now as I was saying, I should get to go first. I started the Woodpushers, remember? It's my board and it was my idea and all."

"Oh, give it a rest, Zimmerman!" David said. "I'm way better at skating vert than you."

"I'm better than both of you," said Henry.

"How about I go first?"

We turned around. It was Mrs. Herschel.

"You?" We looked at her like she was from another planet. Like Uranus.

"In my day I was quite the roller skater," she said. "I even won a trophy when I was a girl."

"You boys should give Mrs. Herschel the first turn," my sister said.

"Yeah," agreed Arcadia, "as a birthday present."

"Uh . . . okay," the three of us agreed. I had never seen an eighty-year-old lady drop into a halfpipe before. But then, in the last three days I had seen a lot of stuff I never thought I'd see.

Julia helped Mrs. Herschel strap on the wooden pads and helmet. I handed her my board.

"Are you goofy or regular?" I asked her.

"I *must* be goofy to do this!" she replied.

As she climbed the ladder up to the top of the halfpipe, the rest of us shouted advice and encouragement.

"You can do it, Mildred!"

"Mrs. Herschel, you are an awesome skater chick!"

"We're going to make you an honorary Woodpusher!"

"Lean forward! Always lean forward!"

Mrs. Herschel positioned the board on the edge of the halfpipe the way we told her to. Then she put a foot on the board and gave us a thumbs-up.

"What is it you Yanks holler before doing something extremely daft?" she asked. "Geronimo?"

"Cowabunga!" suggested Julia, whose skateboarding knowledge comes almost entirely from old episodes of *The Simpsons*. Skating is the only thing I know more about than her.

"Cowabunga!" Mrs. Herschel yelled it as she leaned into the halfpipe.

In a perfect world, Mrs. Herschel would have dropped into the halfpipe, done a 360 flip-to-tailgrab and landed fakie, tearing that thing up like Tony Hawk in his prime. Then we'd give her a standing ovation.

Well, what actually happened was that she fell on her ass.

"Oh, my bum!" she hollered after a spectacular face-plant.

We all came running over, terrified that Mrs. Herschel might have broken her hip or something. But she just dusted herself off and told us we were all a bunch of crybabies.

"Okay," she said, "let's get out of here."

Me and Henry and David took turns skating the halfpipe for about an hour, and it was awesome. Believe me, if you haven't skated the inside shell of a jet plane, you haven't skated. The Canadian police guy was so impressed that he pulled a video camera out of his backpack and filmed us.

We said one last good-bye to our campsite that had been our home. Officer Cavanaugh told us it had been nearly a week since the crash. Somewhere along the way, we had lost track of time. He led us about a mile through the woods to a clearing where a helicopter was waiting to airlift us back to civilization.

That's when things got *really* strange.

I thought our lives were going to return to normal when we got home, but it was just the opposite. When we stepped off the helicopter at the airport, there was a marching band playing and thousands of people cheering. I figured somebody famous must be coming through, but then we realized that somebody was *us*!

It turned out that after our plane crashed, a laptop computer owned by the hijackers was found in the trunk of their rental car which was parked at the airport. It contained documents that showed they were planning to crash the plane into the dome of the United States Capitol, which is nearly three hundred feet above the base of the building. Congress was in session at the time, and, if the hijackers had succeeded, they could have wiped out the United States government!

We also found out that as our plane was coming down, we were traveling almost the length of three football fields every second. If we had been in the air for a few more minutes, we would have smashed into a small town. Who knows how many people would have died?

We weren't just six survivors. We were six heroes in the war on terror.

The day after we were rescued, the video

that Officer Cavanaugh shot of us skating was played over and over again on CNN, MSNBC, *Good Morning America*, the *Today* show, and just about every news program in the world. I guess three guys dressed up like old ladies and skating a halfpipe made out of a downed plane must have captured the interest of the media. Everybody wanted to know all about the Woodpushers.

What happened after that was better than any fantasy I could have dreamed up. Our picture was on the front page of every newspaper in America. We went on *The Tonight Show*. We were invited to the White House. We were honored guests at the X Games. They had a parade for us in New York City. Kids were all over us asking for autographs, like we were real celebrities.

Before the plane crash, all I'd ever wanted was for some skateboard company to sponsor the Woodpushers so we'd get some free T-shirts and boards and stuff. Now, companies were falling all over themselves trying to give us money. Henry got sponsored by some company that paid him a fortune to put his name on helmets and pads that looked like they were made out of tree bark. David signed a deal to endorse an energy drink for extreme athletes.

The girls were heroes too. Arcadia got hired to be the spokesperson for United Airlines. She also received about a million marriage proposals after guys saw her on TV. Julia got a full scholarship to any college in the United States. And she's not even in high school yet! Companies that make laxatives, wheelchairs, denture cream, and other products for senior citizens were tripping all over each other trying to sign up Mrs. Herschel. She was on a reality TV show with Snoop Dogg too.

And me, well, let's just say I did pretty well

for myself. My dad and I patented his titanium skateboard design and we formed a company together called Woodpushers, Inc. I was the star in the Woodpushers TV commercials we shot. Soon kids all over America were buying so many Woodpushers boards that we were having trouble keeping up with the demand. It was sort of like when baseball bats used to be made of wood and then they switched to metal. I'm not allowed to say how much money we've made, but we had to hire a team of accountant guys in suits because there was so much money pouring in that we didn't know what to do with it.

Oh, yeah, one more cool thing happened. This editor from Simon & Schuster Books for Young Readers called me up and asked if I wanted to write a book about the Woodpushers. So I did.

In fact, you just read it.